WHEN ZERO DIED

WHEN ZERO DIED

Sermed Öğretim

New York

Published by Blue Dome Press
535 Fifth Avenue, Ste. 601
New York, NY 10017-8019, USA

www.bluedomepress.com

Library of Congress Cataloging-in-Publication Data Available

ISBN: 978-1-935295-52-5

The majority of the stories first appeared in *The Fountain Magazine*.

Printed by
İmak Ofset, Istanbul - Turkey

TABLE OF CONTENTS

AT THE HEIGHTS OF MOUNT ALPHA

"Since I gained awareness of myself, I have been the owner of this land. With its vast fields, refreshing streams, and friendly animal residents, it has been a part of me. You see those mountains back there? My land starts from their skirts, and extends all the way down to the lake. And behind us are the Great Valley and Eternity Cliffs. You'll appreciate the name given to the cliffs when you see them. Come on let's go."

My journey that weekend started with these sentences from the old man. He was generally calm and content; as if he already found the meaning of his life and what this life could offer him. He was not complaining about what he couldn't do, he was not cursing or talking with remorse about his children. Everything was just calm with this man. His smiling face and his mature spirit very much felt like the sunny blue sky after a night of extreme snow.

"Easy now. When you look down from here, you better cling to someone or something; otherwise, you find yourself in eternity, you know what I mean?" chuckled the old man. So I slowly paced towards the edge of the cliff, but I couldn't see anything because of the clouds covering the view. Realizing that we are actually above the clouds, I exclaimed: "You have this beautiful land up here! Isn't it amazing? This must feel like heaven." Maybe this land explained why he was so content. After all, he had found in the world what many people are trying to find later. He simple replied "maybe..."

Then he took me to the lake side. Unbelievable as it was, the water was warm. "It is always like this. That is why we have a soft climate despite being all the way up here. We have got streams of fresh cold water from the mountains, and we have got the warm water of the lake all year round. I found a hot water source somewhere towards the middle of the lake. You know where that hot water is coming from, right? See! This heaven is sitting on hell. That's why it is a receptacle for inspirations."

After the lake, he took me to the middle of the field. There were different colored flowers in every direction. "This land has the soft climate, and abundant water. It has got a vibrant animal population. And it is fertile enough to grow almost anything you'd like. By choosing your place from the lake to the mountains, you adjust your season. Then you just let it go."

"But I can't see any farming activity here?"

"When I was a small child, I inherited this land from my parents. I don't know what happened to them. I just remember the orphanage I was in for many years. Then, the caregivers found a foster family for me, and we all came to this land. That family, although they didn't do it themselves, contracted the land to other people for farming. During the long years of farming up here, everybody was happy. The farmers raised a good harvest, my foster family received good money, and I had the best childhood memories running up and down the skirts of the mountains with my brothers."

"Then what happened?" I asked curiously.

"Well, as we grew, I developed different interests than my brothers. Instead of running outside, and then playing inside, they ceased the outside fun, and became inside people. They were more TV watching, computer game playing personalities, whereas I stayed outside more and more, climbed higher and higher on the mountains, swam farther into the lake ... Thus, I quickly became capable of managing myself alone. One day, the foster family decided that for the well-being of their kids, and for maintaining the good relations among us, it would be best if they moved down to the city."

"So you've stayed alone since then?"

"At first, yes. But I wasn't quite alone. The farmers kept coming regularly. I have nice memories with the workers. Sometimes they asked me why I did not do other things with the land, since there were so many extraordinary beauties up here. But I did not have the inner power to do such things. And it was actually the farm workers who proposed to me that I meet some travel expert, who would know how to utilize this land for recreation purposes."

"Well, that makes sense. I haven't seen such beauties in my entire life, and so many of them are all together here. If I were you, I would build a huge hotel here, and reap a lot of money."

"Would you? Maybe that's why destiny did not give such a land to you! If you destroy the beauty outside, do you think you can preserve the beauty inside? When there is no beauty inside, your heart becomes blind, and no money can heal it."

I wasn't expecting that response. In fact, I had always had trouble maintaining the beauties in my life. Maybe that was because of my pragmatic character; who knows?

"Don't worry," he continued. "You are not the first business genius appearing here; and you're certainly not the first person to hear words of repulsion from me."

That sounded like a hidden apology. Something was different with this man. His presence awoke respect in me, and his harsh words exposed the rotten smell of my inner world; yet he knew to step back. On one hand, I wanted to get away from him, and on the other, I couldn't help myself staying with him.

"And not everybody stays with me after such words," he added. I asked myself if this man was the same man whom I had initially thought had found heaven in the world. His state now looked more like the lake he showed me. Underneath, a hell; above, a heaven.

"Is that what happened with the travel businessmen?"

"You are intelligent, but too hasty," he said. "They wanted to construct a hotel, but since that would destroy the natural beauty of the land, I proposed making the hotel somewhere below the clouds, and arranging a shuttle service to the summit. They crunched some numbers with their calculators, and discussed some things in private. When they came back, they only said that they were increasing the percentage they are going to give me, but they definitely wanted the hotel at the summit. In other words, they didn't value the beauty at all, other than for its monetary assets."

When the old man described the attitude of the travel businessmen, I wasn't surprised at all, because that was how the business world worked. You don't spend money for conservation until you have to. And if you have a working system that is well established, you just copy-paste it to other places, instead of taking the risk of new systems. Research? Universities do that, and you just purchase it when it is ripe enough. But that mentality certainly did not fit with this old man, who loved the land as a part of his own being.

"So you rejected them!?"

"You know what? No, I accepted their terms with a lease for 3 plus 10 years, three for construction and ten years for running the business. I was naive at the time; I simply thought that they were conducting business, and at the time I did not have a contrasting example to appreciate the value of the land; not to mention my inability to estimate what future visitors were capable of doing in just 10 years."

I wasn't eager to listen to the rest of the story, but I had no choice.

"The hotel was built near the lake. As such, farming activity was restricted to a small area, and that was for exhibition purposes. The contractors made roads everywhere, crossing the fields to reach the mountains. And this land of peace was suddenly filled with people and their noise."

"What happened to you?"

"I? I became a stranger in my own land. The land was contracted for the hotel and was surrounded by metal fence, and even inside, there were rules of conduct. I was locked outside, and very much felt imprisoned."

To escape the weight of the situation, my business genius kicked in, and I inquired: "But they gave you good money, right?"

"Yes, yes. They were honest in that sense, and I gained a good deal of money. In fact, with that money, I had a chance to see the world outside my land. I went to schools in big cities, and learned a lot. I met many wise people, listened to their talks. And most importantly, I visited my foster family regularly, spent time with my brothers. I even had a chance to visit the headquarters of the travel company that was using my land."

"Did you make fun tricks while there? I mean, you acting like a poor man, and them treating you bad, and when they learn about their business with you, suddenly you are treated like a king?"

"Sort of ..."

"What do you mean sort of?"

"I told them that I was looking for a good travel destination, and the officer told about my land as a nice destination. I just kept listening to him, and finally told him that I would like to go somewhere else."

The old man looked like diverging into the depths of his own story, but I was expecting to hear about what happened to the hotel and all those roads.

"By the way, I cannot see a hotel around here. What happened to it?"

"Well, it is exactly where it was constructed; and it is still running."

"Are you making fun of me here? There's not a single entity here taller than 15 meters, and certainly no roads for a busy traffic."

"You know where I went for travel after my little fun at that office? The officer gave me a computer, and using the satellite images, I browsed many places. It just occurred to me to look in detail how my land looked from above, and learn what people said about it. As I zoomed in, I realized that I was living at the summit of a dormant volcano. The hotel was constructed on one side of the crater lake. But the other side of the lake was completely empty. And that's where we are now."

At once, I looked towards the other side of the lake. Behind the haze, I could vaguely spot a gigantic building. Yes, it was really there.

"Years after inheriting it, I became aware of this side of my land, and claimed it as my part of my heaven."

WHEN ZERO DIED

L ong, long ago, in a faraway world inhabited by numbers, it was a clear dawn when the world witnessed the birth of a new number. It was a baby as small as a dot, capable of nothing but crying. They named it Zero. The newborn had no merit at the time, but its presence nonetheless gave joy to life in the realm of numbers. The whole country reverberated with the good news of the birth of Zero.

In caring for baby Zero, the numbers took turns. Each number would hold the baby beside it. As the days passed, the numbers noticed something puzzling. Those numbers who gave care in the right way saw a never-seen abundance at home; everything would increase tenfold. The numbers who passed their turns superficially did not see any difference. Was it a sign from God that the numbers could not grasp?

The days went by, and the numbers expected to see developments in the newborn. It was supposed to make facial expressions, start uttering some meaningful sounds, make purposeful movements with its arms, and so on. But zero did not exhibit any of the expected qualities. The numbers thought maybe it was a late-bloomer. But soon they began to understand that this number was disabled. It did not seem to give any known response to the stimuli. It would not make a difference when used in addition or subtraction games. In the multiplication game, it would give a deep silence as the result, no matter how big a number it played with. And in the division game, no matter what number divided Zero, the result would be a hopeless reluctance to change. The numbers could not reconcile the miraculous abundance that showed up with the proper care for Zero, with its extraordinary disability. What was the deal with this baby?

Years flew by like the water in a stream, and Zero entered adolescence. Its body was growing very fast and was also assuming a more rounded shape, leaving its primitive, seed-like dot form. With the rebellious instincts of adolescence, Zero discovered its ability to roll, instead of the step-by-step walk of the others. And soon it discovered that it was able to move much faster than the others by rolling. This unexpected burst of motor skills from Zero made the numbers very happy. They did not have to put burden themselves anymore to move Zero. Once a totally disabled baby, Zero was now the fastest member in the numbers kingdom, which even the wealthiest numbers could not catch up with.

The downside of this was that Zero was not able to stop. To stop, it had to hit another number, just like in the multiplication game. Perhaps the wisdom in the apparent disability of Zero at the beginning of its life was that it needed to learn the wisdom to control its extraordinary moving ability later in life. But in the first months of its new skill, Zero just rolled, rolled and rolled. Even accidents did not scare Zero from its attempts to roll farther and faster. Considering its long years of immobility, that's all the justification it needed,

As Zero continued to grow, with the other numbers watching closely, they noticed an interesting feature. Due to its perfect symmetry, Zero possessed an enthralling beauty. How is it possible that such unparalleled elegance emerged in a number initially considered disabled? The numbers decided to consult the Savant One. One was the oldest of the numbers, was held to be noble, and knew history very well. As knowledgeable and dignified as it was, One was also humble, bending its torso low to talk with children, instead of raising its head straight up.

Savant One said, "I have been reading the ancient books about the signs of this number. As it was foretold, it was born disabled, and it was raised by its relatives; it then surpassed everyone by its speed and its perfect symmetry. As Zero grows, it is assuming the shape that we observe in all heavenly objects. The youngest member of our community has more to teach us. We must wait and see."

After the numbers had left the house of One, Prime Minister Two could not hold back, and raised its voice: "Could it be that the old guy is mixing things up? I mean, how do we know that the things written in those old books are authentic? Zero is not so different from us; it is just another number. Why are we bothering ourselves with something that no one has seen before? Are we going to leave the greatest numbers for the sake of this fledgling egg?" Then Two burst into laughter. Some of the numbers joined in, while others said, "We'll see!"

As the years passed, Zero started questioning its existence, and contemplating its character as a number. It had heard the words of both the Savant One and the Prime Minister Two, but it could not come to a satisfying conclusion. Maybe Two was right. Even if the ancient books did talk about someone special to come, who said that it was Zero? With this mind-set, Zero preferred a middle way between that of Savant One and that of Prime Minister Two.

As Zero was leaving adolescence, something started bothering it from within. It was as if somebody were periodically disturbing its comfort by triggering emotions that were dissatisfied with the stuff of daily life. Zero started reflecting again. It considered all it had experienced thus far in its unusual life story: its initial disability and the consequent burst of motor skills, its initial negligible size and the unparalleled beauty it exhibited as it grew, the words of the Savant One and those of Prime Minister Two, and so on.

At that moment, Zero felt a sudden shiver, with the coolness of an inspiration that penetrated its whole body. Zero felt that its life was full of opposites, and by pondering the respective non-existence and existence of its qualities, it might understand infinity. These thoughts motivated Zero to investigate infinity by talking to other numbers.

The answer that best resonated with what Zero felt was from Savant One: "I have not seen infinity, but I do know that I was the first one to exist among numbers. I feel that I could not have come to be out of nothing. Seeing all these numbers that came after me, I understand that what made me is infinity. Oh, my little one, if you ask what was one step before me, the ancient books say it is you who will reveal that." The answer that Zero did not like was from the Prime Minister Two: "There is no such thing as infinity. No matter how great a number you imagine, by adding one, you can always obtain a greater number. This is all there is to it; there is no one who has actually seen infinity, anyway; it is no more than a figment of our imagination."

When alone, Zero thought, "I can understand Two because when it came to the world, it saw One already there; so, Two cannot comprehend coming to existence without an ancestor. But what I feel inside is more like what One tells me. One can feel the existence of something that triggered its existence because when it came to the world, there was none other than One." After a silence, Zero mumbled, "If I exist, then you exist. But where are you? If only I could see you…"

Life had been very turbulent for Zero. First, disabilities burdened it, then a sudden explosion of skills and emotions moved it, then a painful questioning without satisfactory answers shook it, and finally a conclusion that brought peace along with a wish for homecoming. Soon after, not being able to stand the harshness of such turbulence, Zero fell sick. It started losing weight to the point that it almost returned to its seed-like state at birth. With this harrowing sickness at such a young age, Zero had suffered enough.

Although everybody was saddened, they thought that it was best for this unique number to die.

And Zero died. They buried it under the quotient line. Roses grew on its grave that were as beautiful as Zero, as noble as One. Thus was commemorated the phrase "one over zero," in order to refer to this beauty. It was only then that the numbers understood what Zero felt inside. The numbers visited Zero from time to time, whenever they needed a glimpse of beauty stretching from infinity. As powerless as it was, Zero helped others understand infinity not by its existence among them, but by lying below them.

INTERVIEW WITH THE TWO LOBES OF BRAIN

Moderator: Good evening, ladies and gentlemen. Tonight, we have two guests that have long been the focus of attention in the media: Left Brain and Right Brain. We are going to discuss with them their opinions on various issues. Without losing much time, I want to get to the first question. Many public figures who inspired people have a period of self-discovery, after which they define their identities and their surroundings anew. Did you have a similar self-discovery period? And if yes, how do you define yourself now?

Left Brain: I guess I never had a distinct enlightenment period, but I kept building on top of what I already knew about myself. So, my self-discovery starts with my babyhood, really. For example, as my eyes gained the ability to distinguish colors and to focus on objects at different distances, I realized that I can collect information about the outside world through colors, shapes, and distances. As the muscles became stronger, I felt free to move my body and developed the notion of being distinct from other things around me. I also realized that I can gather data about what is where, how I can find what I need … When I learned to speak, I developed the notion that there are other people like me out there, for whom I am the other. And so on …

Right Brain: Before I say anything, I would like to bring to your attention that the way I am named is not something I came up with nor something I am delighted with. For me, there isn't a left-right distinction. There is a brain, and that's it. And actually, I would not call the eyes as different organs. They are only a different part of the same organ, i.e. the brain. Muscles are alike. They are not distinct entities. We are all part of the same organ. So, for me too, self-discovery started with my babyhood, but realizing my new abilities forced me to redefine myself again and again. For example, when I discovered my legs,

I did not become a brain with legs, but opened my eyes into a new dimension of my existence. I realized that I was not just about what I thought I was. The same goes for vision, smell. So, when you smell something for the first time, that is a creative act. When you taste a fruit for the first time ever, that is an invention for you. All these culminate in a notion in which everything unifies. Walking is thinking, thinking is walking. Seeing is tasting, tasting is seeing. So, for example, if you cannot solve a problem, try smelling it, tasting it, walking it.

Left Brain: Let's not get poetic here. If you cannot solve a problem, that's because you either haven't gathered enough data or haven't got a known pattern of solution. It is also possible that you are suffering from attention deficit at that moment due to distractions such as walking, smelling, tasting; you know what I mean?

Moderator: Let's not lose our focus here. The next topic I want to bring forward is a little more subtle: love and marriage. What do you think is love, and why are marriages today more restrained than before?

Left Brain: There are different categories of love. The love between couples and the love between the parents and their children, and then the love between friends ... these are not the same. So I am assuming that you are specifically talking about the one between couples. Even in this type of love, there are various facets. Sometimes it means dedication to support each other, sometimes it is being valued by the other. You can extend this list. Love is like light. The same phenomenon can display itself in different colors and strength. Today, there is much research going on about the physical manifestations of love, and the properties of successful marriages. There are also studies on divorces. It seems that, for the moment, there is no predictor of the fate of a given marriage in the long run. Having said that, I should admit that there are some symptoms of an imminent divorce, such as regular alcohol consumption, having divorced friends, and extended periods without intimacy. The more of these you have, the more likely are you to face a divorce in the first five or ten years of your marriage. Aside from the factors that are related to the conscience of the individuals, there are more subtle factors that need extra focus. The fast pace of change in modern life versus the slow-changing cultural settings definitely brings stress to many couples.

The norms and expectations from each other depend on one's cultural and emotional baggage. Whether one can fulfill those expectations given the modern conditions is another story. All these are playing a role in the restriction of the family in our times.

Right Brain: Like anything else in the universe, we look for unity. If you love someone, you want to be with them, because love is a realization that part of your existence is in the other. We all crave to be one with those we love. But why do we feel such emotions only for one person, and not just for anyone? Perhaps, this is one of the points where the veils before destiny are pulled open. When we tell someone that we love them, we actually mean, "I need you ... and I need to be needed." This is a two-way hunger which is quenched by the unity of the lovers. This is why love inherently demands continuity; for unity is only established when all separations in time and space are eliminated. And this is why, perhaps, marriages are most troubled today. Life conditions and individual choices are not made in order to nourish the continuity. Staying side by side is mistaken for unity.

Moderator: Have you ever fallen in love?

Left Brain: Is there anyone who hasn't? As one colleague of mine says: "we are wired for love and belonging; that's why we are here." Love is one way of becoming a part of something bigger than us. Having a family, raising children, and contributing to the well-being of our society through various love-inspired activities. Even ascetics and saints pursue a path of love inspired by God. So, love is all around us.

Moderator: But I asked if you ever "fell in love"? I understand if you don't want to go that deep into your private life.

Left Brain: (pauses for a second) … I might have felt special things for some people. But, in the long run, I saw that those feelings did not bear any meaning for the real life. And this realization gained me immunity towards those special feelings. If you can stand back, and take a deep breath … Oh yes, and let me say this as an aside: This is how love works. You cannot stay away from the situation and breathe deeply so that you cannot think clearly. Love only works when you can't think clearly. This loss of brain power is eliminated when you hit the bottom of the love you are falling in. So, what was I saying? If you stand back and take a deep breath, you'll see that there are thousands of people with whom you can get along with at least as well as the one you are facing at that moment. Nobody is irreplaceable. There is always another one more beautiful, friendlier, more generous, more sacrificing, etc. There is always going to be another love following the current one. So, no need for falling!

Moderator: What about you, Right Brain? Have you ever fallen in love?

Right Brain: I can't breathe without love! For me, life and everything in it gains meaning only through love. And this meaning is not always visible to the eyes at first sight. "L'essentiel est invisible pour les yeux. On ne voit bien qu'avec le cœur." As the fox tells the Little Prince, what's essential is invisible to the eye; one only sees well with their hearts. So, falling in love reveals the meanings hidden behind objects and events. It's not that you fall in love with something that is extraordinary, but that love makes the ordinary things extraordinary. It is the intertwining of their destinies that make people special for each other. Imagine this: the Great Author of the universe is writing a love story of you and your beloved one. What greater meaning can you ask for? For me, each and every person I fell in love with is special, no matter how the story ended. I always keep a room reserved for them in my heart.

Moderator: In the last century, scientific thought and technological achievements led many people to question their religious teachings and affiliations. Their faiths were shaken as a result of their experiences in the intellectual and social areas. I even remember a book titled "youth's faith is stolen by questions." My question to you is, how do you define the relationship between religion and science?

Left Brain: This question was asked at many other occasions. For me, this is a straightforward issue. Personally, I am a believer. For me, science gathers information about the outside world. Religion tells me the purpose of the world. A more cliché way of saying the same thing is, "science answers how, religion answers why." Therefore, I don't see why the two should contradict or clash. You can have a user's manual for a car or a computer. But what you are going to do with it is totally up to you. Science and technology are like that manual. From them, we learn to make use of what is available here in this world. But religion guides us in what we should do, or how we should do it.

Right Brain: If you go back in history, you'll see that religion and science were not different entities. Even the several branches of science we have today were united into a single body. If you were a knowledgeable man, you knew everything. Of course, with the accumulation of more and more information, a classification was needed, but unfortunately this classification led to the separation of these different classes. Nowadays, people are rediscovering the value of unity of knowledge through the interdisciplinary studies. The same, I think, is true for religion and science. Had things taken a different route in history, one in which the sense of unity was essential, the definitions we are using today in our talk would have been completely different. Science would not be the study of how universe functions, but how God executes his will in the physical realm. Similarly, instead of being perceived as a set of rules that bound both God and people, the laws of nature would be defined as the stable patterns (straight paths) of creation that host travelers in life. Accordingly, those stable paths would be a restriction for us, humans, but not for the Lord of the worlds. Such an understanding would have, perhaps, fostered a completely different history than what we have now. Reading creation as verses from the Perfect Designer, treating life events as personal instant messages from the closest Friend ... these things would transform our journey in this world from a merciless struggle of survival to being the hero of our life stories that are co-authored by the Supreme Sustainer.

The same goes for how religion is perceived and practiced throughout many centuries. Instead of drying out to a set of precise number of certain actions and words, religion would be the way to educate our conscience and will in order to be respectful lovers of God. Instead of becoming a formula that "ensures" heaven solely for its followers, religion would be the means to spread peace and prosperity to everyone, just like the All-Merciful one sustains even those who deny His existence.

Moderator: Finally, I would like to ask you the ultimate question. Where is the world headed with its current turbulences in economy, health, and politics? Do you see hope in the future?

Left Brain: Oh, absolutely! People have been voicing similar issues for a long time. Even when the world population was a third of what it is now, there were debates on whether food would be enough, and so on ... But today, we are here with a population of 7 billion. It may be painful, but I am sure in the long run, things will get settled.

Moderator: Painful? What do you mean by that?

Left Brain: Of course there are wars for many reasons, and there is a disparity in the distribution of wealth, and healthcare is not accessible in many places. So, it is going to take some time until a global welfare and healthcare system is established to cover everyone. But with the advent of technology in communications and transportation, this is going to become easier in time, and we'll get there. Until that point, though, there are going to be losses.

Right Brain: There is an old saying: "If He didn't want to give, He wouldn't give the desire." I think the fact that we are yearning for a better tomorrow is a sign that we'll get there.

Moderator: Then, would you blame the turbulence today to yesterday's lack of desire for better tomorrows?

Right Brain: You are making me smile. Desire for a better tomorrow is not the same thing as desire for better income. If everybody dreams for a better tomorrow, then this becomes a global prayer for peace and prosperity. If everybody wants what's best for themselves, they don't add up. Worse, if some people think of their prosperity at the expense of others. So, in this sense, I think we can talk about a lack of desire for a better tomorrow, which governed the world for most of the last century. Today, though, through the growing means of communication and transportation, interfaith-intercultural dialogue activities are sprouting. These carry the potential to initiate a global prayer for peace and prosperity. When that happens, I am hopeful that that prayer will be answered.

Moderator: Thank you Left Brain and thank you Right Brain for allowing us to have a peek into your personal worlds.

THE LAST PRAYER FOR GIANTS

L ong, long ago, before the end of time, I heard a legendary story from my grandpa about what happened between him and a giant unlike other giants...

It was around dawn, and the day was not yet fully light. Rain the night before had left a thick cloud cover. The music of bugs and the chanting of birds filled the air. A slight breeze provided a smooth and continuous whistle, and consecutive, rhythmic thumps could be heard. The thumps were the sounds of a giant's footsteps as he walked to work early in the morning.

Meanwhile, my grandpa and his friends were enjoying the water on a walkway. A hot day was soon going to turn this walkway into a deathbed for many of his friends. Along with the day's heat, the footsteps of the giants would crush the lives of many others. But neither he nor his friends were aware of this. They were simply enjoying their water on the walkway.

That fateful morning, the giant bent down toward my grandfather, grabbed a thin stick from the ground, and tried to kill him. Not prepared for such an attack in the midst of his breakfast, my grandfather was stupefied, and did not know what to do. He barely spiraled away, as we always do in case of danger, to escape the giant's attack. But it was in vain; the giant would not give up.

Finally, the giant accomplished his mission, and my grandfather was saved from both the heat and the giant footsteps. It turned out that my grandpa had misunderstood the giant. Many other giants would walk on us, or ignore us, and this giant was the same; or so he had thought. But this one was trying to put the stick under my grandpa to lift him and place him onto the soil where he could be safe. My grandpa said that he later appreciated this help even more, when he heard of his friends dying on that same walkway.

The story of a giant unlike others of his kind spread through family to friends and became known everywhere. The world underground rejoiced at the existence of a selfless giant. Perhaps there were other giants like him. The underground world kept praying for those giants, that they might be protected from things of which they were unaware, just as that special giant had saved my grandfather from unknown dangers.

After my grandfather's time, his story became a nostalgic tale for the elders, and a bedtime story for little ones. Over time, the world aboveground became worse than the world underground. Instead of long trees above with their roots underground, there were huge, tall rocks in both places. The rocks underground provided water to everyone, but the rocks aboveground provided water only to the giants. The roots of the plants and trees used the marrow of the earth to improve it, but the long channels that the giants sank into the ground were like huge veins, draining the earth to death. We ceased praying for them.

One day, we heard screaming among the giants about an asteroid heading directly toward the earth. The only thing they were worried about was the end of their own lives. We were not surprised by this selfish reaction to that event because of their selfish behavior on the earth. And the asteroid came…

It was foggy again, but not because of clouds; it was quite dark, but there would be no dawn. The fog and the darkness were from dust spread over the face of the earth. We were fortunate to sustain our lives under such harsh conditions. As for the giants, they were not suffering much from the conditions, as the survivors had taken shelter in special chambers built only for them. We were of significant use to them. After using the entire earth selfishly, now they went about enslaving us. They still lacked our prayers for their protection. Could they ever understand, in their hardened hearts, why such tragedy had befallen them?

Not long after that, we witnessed something incredible. One of the giants came out of the protection chambers to do something completely unexpected. He looked through his goggles at the sky and tried to take a deep breath. As he was coughing because of the dust in the air, he opened the nylon bag he was carrying. He sat on the ground, dug a hole with his hands, and uncovered the thing in the bag: a daisy plant. Was he going to plant it? But why? The chances of its survival were nearly zero. What benefit would it bring him even if it survived for a day? And yet, he looked pleased by what he was doing. He even smiled at a worm that was escaping the hole he had made. What was going on in his mind?

Just at the moment, the earth suddenly started shaking violently. The planet was dying because of the deep cracks caused by the impact of the asteroid. Neither the giant nor the flower had any chance of survival. He did not know what to do for a moment, then he burst into tears: "Oh my God! Oh my God!"

He saw the deep cracks forming near him, shaking and growing. It was as if the planet had started shouting at him in thousands of voices. He could not stand up to the quaking and fell down next to the hole, as if it were he, not the flower, that would be planted in it. At that moment, the giant was no different from us: lying on the ground, seeking his way out of certain doom. Who was there to help him? His cries became screams: "Oh my God! Oh my God!"

All of a sudden, he stopped crying and started talking to someone, though we could not see anybody around: "Please, hold me tight. Do not leave me…." He continued, "But I can't… I can't…." Feebly, he tried to reach the flower that had fallen from his hands. He cradled it against his chest; but at that moment he was struck by a stone and he fell unconscious. As he was sinking into the growing cracks, we uttered a prayer for the giant who had planted a flower in his heart… The last prayer of worms, the last prayer for giants…

STAFF ONLY!

I t was an ordinary day. As usual, I was sleepy. I had not had enough rest, since I was on call the previous night. Right before lunch, I was making plans about how I could sneak into the attractive "staff only" dining room and take a little nap. If there was one thing I learned in the few years of training, it was that there is nothing comparable to a good nap for lunch. Again, as usual, I made a meticulous diagnosis of the hallway and the entrance to the dining room: All signs were "go." In the room, what would be a nicer companion than some classical music? And Vivaldi's *The Four Seasons* filled my ears— my cell phone was ringing. I was expected in the emergency room. How much could it hurt, if I only took a few minutes of sleep? Sigh …

The man had only fallen unconscious, but his family thought he had had a heart attack and brought him to emergency. The initial diagnosis was that his artery was almost clogged up due to cholesterol, and the doctor on duty decided to follow a clean-up procedure. This would be my seventh time in a similar operation, so I was not really nervous. But in the eyes of the patient's family, I saw panic. They were screaming for help, and watching them made my eyes almost deaf when I finally managed to throw myself into the surgery room. Oh my comfort zone: staff only.

As the operation started, the serpentine cord that carried the visualization instrument gradually made its way towards the patient's heart. The walls of the arteries were covered with black remains, fatty tissues were hanging down here and there, and minor clogs had built up at sharp turns. I remembered my dad, who was a plumber. Many times, he was called into the "staff only" rooms for clogged pipes. In contrast to my love for them, the "staff only" rooms were his nightmare. "Poor dad", I thought, pitying him, even if it was thirty years later.

"Go on," came an unknown voice, waking me up from my childhood memories. "Where," I asked in my mind. Then I realized that the camera was showing inside the heart. Looking from within, it only made sense that the man fell unconscious. How could such a heart support the demands of a body?

"He probably hasn't had a refreshing breath for a long time, and certainly wasn't able to run with his grandchildren," I murmured.

"He never did that anyway, so that he should suffer from not doing it now!" answered the unknown voice.

"This is not the time to critique. He is in our hands, waiting for help," I replied.

"Well, do what you can. Even if you can fix the entrance, you won't be able to fix me. By the way, would you like a drink?"

Wasn't that a kind heart? Learning who my host was, I rejoiced despite the stress. With the heavy illumination in the surgery room, I was in fact terribly hot at that moment—as if helping my mom while cooking in the kitchen. "Yes, please, a cold drink would quench my heat," I accepted.

"I am sorry, but I only serve hot drinks here. Cold drinks are served in dead bodies," teased the heart. "Here is your energy drink."

"WHAATTT?" I spat all that was in my mouth, and threw the cup towards the heart. The same instant, I received the words of disdain: "Did you just make a heart attack?"

"You are, sir, sucking the man's blood," I replied in anguish.

"That is what's available in here," answered the heart teasingly. "I have production wells extending throughout his body, and I drink this warm energy drink constantly. Without it, I cannot live. If I cannot live, he cannot live. So it is a win-win situation, you know what I mean?"

"Wait a minute, aren't you the embodiment of love and compassion? Aren't you supposed to give without a return?"

"That is true, indeed so. But there is another condition on the same agreement, which says that I have all the rights to defend myself if my carrier denies my rights of privacy."

A heart defending its privacy from its carrier! I was as bewildered and as silenced as a fetus going through birth. The heart took my confused pause as a request for explanation.

"My carrier developed a habit of welcoming thieves as if guests into me, and they kept robbing me," cried the heart, collapsing. "After a while, I decided to separate myself from him, even if that meant the end of my life. The first thing to win my independence was not to use his blood. So, I started narrowing the artery that was feeding me. After all, I was doing something I was familiar with: giving without taking. That rendered me weaker; but he became weaker, too. With his health gone, no thieves were interested in him anymore. And I was safe from both my carrier and the thieves."

Strained between anger and affection, my breaths became deeper and stronger. For relief, I turned my head around. Then suddenly, I started shaking from what I happened to see. "What is this door," I managed to ask at last.

"Don't you see the sign? It is a room for staff only."

"Staff only!" I smiled as if I had found water in desert. But after realizing that I wouldn't be able to go in there, I went through a storm of sentiments: outcast, unable, sad.

"You feel distanced, right?" asked the heart, to which I nodded.

"That sign is there so that the grown-ups don't enter. If you were a child, you would not be able to read it, and would directly rush in without asking."

"Why children only?" I inquired.

"If you can go through this door in your heart, you can get out into the heart of another person. And if you are a grown-up at that moment, you are going to be treated like a thief in that heart. But if you are a child, you are going to be welcomed as a guest."

I listened to the heart, waited at front of the door. I thought about the people in my life, especially those with whom I wanted to be closer. This door could be the key. I raised my hand, held the door knob. But then I thought about what I was going to face on the other side. Was I entering as a child? Or was I an ambitious adult who was going to be treated as a thief? It was also possible that my grown-up state could trigger the heart on the other side to react to its carrier just like this one; and that would mean trouble for one of my loved ones ...

I certainly was not staff ... I stepped back from that door, as if waking from a pleasurable dream that I did not want to leave. Then, the heart gently told me: "Go upstairs to the kitchen, now; you are expected to open a clogged pipe."

A SATURDAY UNLIKE OTHERS

Many of us either heard about or read Antoine de Saint-Exupéry's The Little Prince. The hero of the story sets out on a journey that will take him to several planets on which he meets people who are representative of different characters. The purpose of his journey is to make new friends and to find answers to the question why. In other words, he is trying to understand the meaning of his life. During this journey, he meets a fox that teaches him two secrets related to the answer of his subconscious question. The story ends with the Little Prince dying from a serpent bite. However, his apparent death is only a transformation so that he can leave his body, which is too heavy for the journey on which he is now setting out. This journey is his homecoming, and we listen to his memories after his arrival.

On a Friday evening, the Little Prince land-ed on his home planet. He went to his precious rose and related his travel stories to her…

"And I saw so many flowers with different colors on the earth."

After few forced coughs, the rose responded jealously:

"But were they as beautiful as me?"

"There were many roses just like you; but I learned that you are unique…"

"Then go talk with them. If you are not go-ing to water me with your words, telling me how much you missed me, why did you come here at all?"

These were the last words of the rose, as it had not been watered for some time. The death of his rose, his only friend at home, shook the Little Prince to his core. As his home planet was so small, his tears soon became a lake. He de-cided to bury his rose near this lake, the lake that sprang from his heart.

At the end of the day, he sat by the lake and watched the sunset. Then he remembered his conversations with the fox. The fox had said that if they became friends, he would cry after the Little Prince departed. And he would stare at the golden glow of the wheat fields, for their yellow hue would remind him of his blond friend, the Little Prince.

Taking the fox's words to heart, the Little Prince decided to assign meanings to the things around him to remind him of his rose. The scarlet of the sky at sunset became the petals of the rose, the wings of the birds became its leaves. Most importantly, the lake of his tears became his love for his precious one. Whenever the Little Prince wanted to remember his rose, he came to the lakeside at sunset, stared at the horizon as the sun colored the sky with the petals of his rose, and he added more tears to his lake of love.

On one such day, he felt the absence of his rose so strongly that he cried aloud, sobbing deeply. "Everything comes to an end, just like the sun, just like my rose…" With these words, a shockwave reverberated in his mind: What about my own end? This question brought others, like a chain reaction: Is it possible to know when his life was going to end? What would happen afterwards? What is the meaning of all

the manifest beauties if they are destined to perish? What is the wisdom behind love, if it leads
to so much destruction in the heart upon separation?

Then he remembered the two secrets that
the fox had shared with him: 1) It is only with
the heart that one can see well, for the essential
is invisible to the eye, 2) it is the time that you
spend with your rose that makes her so important to you. He thought "the essence of my rose
cannot be mere soil; the essence of my love cannot be only tears…" Did this mean that if he
wanted to see his rose, he could see her with his
heart? Or, was the time with his rose spent in
vain, since she had departed without considering the sorrow of the Little Prince?

Days passed with unanswered questions like
these. The Little Prince looked at the sheep in
the box drawn by the pilot on the earth. He
sighed, and wished that the sheep could get
out of their home; the absence of his friend had
slowly but surely destroyed him. Seeing that his
desire for company was not realized, he slowly
lost his hope. He was too aware of his own doom
in his soul. But, within the shadowy depths of

his heart, one question kept him alive: When he was lost in the desert with the pilot, with no water left, how did they happen to find a water well exactly when they were most in need of it? Out of the infinite number of ways they could have followed, were they guided by a hidden hand to the particular path that lead to the well?

Whenever the Little Prince thought about this moment, he felt the warmth of unseen company. Perhaps this was something he could see with his heart, but not with his eyes. He wanted to call this essence that he could see with his heart the essence of life. He reasoned that if the essence of life had not loved him, it would have abandoned him to perish in the desert. "I love you, too," he whispered. Then he continued to talk to the essence of life; maybe it would hear him, and respond to his need. And with this final thread of hope to be delivered from misery, the Little Prince had conversations with the essence of life that he could not see. He tried to have his conversations at the same time of the day, as the fox had told him. The more time he spent with the essence of life, the closer he felt to it, just like the fox had told him. He felt that he was making a new friend, finding love again. The feeling of being taken care of was indescribably comforting.

One day, while he was walking by the lake, he came to the place where he had buried his rose the year before. He started to cry. As his tears dropped on the graveyard, the Little Prince silently whispered, "My precious rose, I cannot see you, but I do believe in the essence that my heart feels. It is the time that I spent with you that made you so important to me. And it is my entire life that makes me so important to the essence of life. I feel something extraordinary, because I feel that the essence of life loves me. I am sure it is taking care of you as well, and I feel that I am going to see you again."

After his last sentence, he felt something inside that he could not put into words; a feeling of serenity blended with a glimpse of reunion. But how, when, and where? These questions were unanswered. It was as if his mind were imprisoned in a cell, while his heart was rejoicing at the new freedom that it found within the very essence of life. Since his mind could not keep up with his heart, and he fell asleep from the intense conflict between the two.

The Little Prince did not visit his rose for a long time after that. One Saturday morning, he woke up as the dawn was glazing the surface of the lake of love. He went to the lakeside and washed his face with its water. Then behold! He saw his rose bursting forth from the soil where he had buried her the previous year.

STORM OF CHANGE

It was one of the first days of spring when a butterfly appeared in our forest. She was so charming with her vibrant blues, yellows, and blacks that everyone wanted to be close to her. In order to attract her for a chat, the trees displayed their most beautiful leaves and flowers, but to no avail. Eventually, the butterfly fluttered her elegant wings through our forest, approaching a select few to make conversation. In a soft, sweet voice, the butterfly asked if we, the young trees of the forest, would like to hear her story. I was one of those chosen to listen.

"You know, I wasn't always like this," began the butterfly. "I used to creep on the ground instead of flying in the air. I used to have gloomy colors and obnoxiously long hair instead of these lovely colors and elegant wings."

It was really hard for me to believe that the butterfly had ever been as she described. I am sure the other fellows in our group were also surprised to hear this, but none of us wanted to interrupt the flow of her beautiful words.

"My situation back then troubled me, indeed. Why was I doomed to get smashed under the feet of others? Why was beauty innate to other creatures while ugliness was my fate? Dissatisfied with my situation, I wanted to change, dreamed of waking up into a new day, longed to breathe the air of a fresh life. My creeping ugly body did not match my spirit within."

At this point, I couldn't hold back anymore, and asked: "So what did you do about it? Was it then that you turned into this beautiful state?" The butterfly reacted most unexpectedly to my question. She neither smiled nor gave a humble answer. Without changing the expression on her face, she continued, as if she hadn't heard me: "I couldn't do anything about it." Then she stopped speaking. You know how long intermissions like this can feel. After a few moments, the butterfly became serious, as if she had a duty to tell her story, not praise herself.

"In my desperation, I decided to bring all this to an end. I slowly climbed a high tree. From that height, the scene looked very different. I was able to observe things from above, just like the birds. I had found a security and serenity that I could never find on the ground. It was the perfect day to begin my change. If I wanted to be revived anew, I needed to die first."

We weren't expecting to hear such words from our unique guest. Why was she telling us all this anyway? We were young trees looking forward to our bright futures. The gloom in her words veiled her beauty, and eclipsed our interest in listening to her. Noticing the change in our facial expressions, the butterfly continued:

"And slowly, I started tying the rope that I carefully made myself, and rendered myself to the hands of the wind. And just like I had predicted, things started changing very quickly as I descended towards the ground. I realized something that I had never thought before: I belonged to someone who did not want me to perish like this. It was as if time suddenly stopped, and I had a chance to communicate with my Owner. I was ashamed of what I had done, and asked for a second chance, which was given to me. Then I came to find myself hanging from the tree."

I was thinking that the butterfly was going to conclude with "hanging from the tree in this vibrant beauty." Astonishingly, there was more to the story of how she gained this beauty. My interest started to build up again, and I observed the same curiosity on my friends' faces.

"In my anguish and shame, I started covering my body. I wove a small tent around myself. I was alone in my darkness, away from the insults, from the harassments, and from myself. During my retreat, I tried to re-evaluate things, and think about positive ways to change. After a while, I decided to rid myself of my cocoon and do something. But there was one hurdle: I was hanging down in the middle of the air, covered with an intricately woven house. I had to undo the excellent job I had done, but it wasn't easy to tear apart my silken prison.

"As small pieces of the house were torn, and I was able to glimpse the daylight, I tried even harder and more urgently to free myself. When the hole was large enough, I squeezed myself through. Reflected in the puddle below me, it was at that moment that I saw my new self. I gave the most heartfelt praise to my Owner."

This was the butterfly's story of change. She admonished us to make positive changes in our lives and in ourselves. She also talked about how potent our bodies are in facilitating change.

This was wholeheartedly embraced in our forest by the young trees, including me. Why? Because we were in the very same place where we were born; so we wanted to do something about it. We were inspired by the butterfly's story and decided to mobilize ourselves. Even the peaceful nights, formerly filled with the rhythmic voices of crickets, were now teeming with the whispers of our discussions on how to enact this fundamental change.

No wonder the old trees found this activity among the young outrageous and inappropriate. They thought we were trying to go against our nature. The time spent on these efforts was regarded as a waste. The old trees first tried to warn us against our "hallucinations," but it turned out to be a fruitless effort. Then the old trees threatened to block our sunlight by covering us from above. This, too, was disregarded when the old trees realized their sanctions would kill their young ones instead of changing their minds. In the meantime, our ideas caught the attention of the newer generations. Upon hearing the whole story regarding the butterfly and our efforts to change, they too joined in our desire to mobilize. Eventually, the old trees decided to wait and see what would happen. After all, we were simply trying to imitate the butterfly.

Ever since that spring when the butterfly shared her story, we all covered ourselves with as many leaves as possible, similar to the cocoon of the butterfly. We were hoping that when the autumn winds blew those leaves away, our mobilized inner selves would emerge, like the initial flight of the butterfly. We persistently covered ourselves this way year after year, but neither did our roots become feet, nor did our branches become wings. Eventually, we realized we were merely getting older, and that we were wasting our time. No one could advise us, either, because the butterfly had died that same long-ago spring, and the older trees had long ago shunned us because of our stubborn foolishness.

Once young trees, we were now experienced and mature, so we decided to talk about the failed plan that was meant to lead us to change.

Instead of reciting the misleading story of the butterfly, we would talk about why this had happened to us, and how we should advise our young. We started by analyzing the cautions of the old trees. Although we were not fully able to comprehend the wisdom of the elders, we could sense the implicit good in their words.

As our voices undulated in the air, a migrating bird heard us and made a swift landing nearby. She quickly spoke up: "You know, we also had a problem amongst our young, but it was in the opposite direction. They wanted to quit traveling and stay in one place. We even lost some of them last winter when they decided not to migrate." The unexpected interruption by the bird brought other questions to mind. Why was this problem always occurring with the young? Why did they fancy a nature opposite to their own? We couldn't come to a conclusion.

One day, a short time after the discussion with the bird, we witnessed a mobile tree and a stationary bird. The tree was being carried behind a huge animal making a horrible, obnoxious noise, an animal we had never seen. To our surprise, the two men riding the animal had also captured a bird, and somehow turned her into a stationary bird that could constantly stand on the walls surrounding their home. Neither the mobile tree nor the stationary bird created joy in the forest.

The mobilization of trees and the immobilization of birds continued until one day there were hardly any trees or birds left. Something was terribly wrong; none of this had brought any good to our forest. The few remaining trees wanted to stay where they were born, and the few remaining birds wanted to fly.

Spring had once been breezy and warm, but now on an unusually hot spring day, a butterfly appeared in the place where our forest used to be. She carried a poetry book she had composed. As the butterfly voiced her yearning for the glorious trees in the land and the soaring birds in the skies, tears of regret filled our eyes. And her verses of nostalgia ended with a prayer:

Oh the Unchanging One despite the transients,
Oh the Eternal One in the face of all mortals,
Oh the Creator of all animals that are now only in the tales,
Resurrect nature, we implore with our silence.

IN AN AUTHOR'S MIND

Rational, Romantic, and Regular were three roommates. They were new writers with splendid ambitions. They dreamt of one day displaying the best of their talents. To achieve this, they had different writing styles and strategies. Rational, who had graduated from the school of science, always sought a sound reason for writing, and did not schedule a time for writing otherwise. Romantic, on the other hand, had no formal education. But she had been well-trained by her parents as a keen observer of the material and spiritual realms. Romantic reserved ample time to wait for inspiration and to dress it in the most beautiful words whenever it came. Regular, a graduate of a military school, split his days into well-defined slots, and had a regular time for writing.

Reductionist, their next-door neighbor, was editor-in-chief of a well-known magazine. He was older, and had a rather fatherly attitude toward them. Not surprisingly, each of the three writers had one thing in mind: to catch the attention of their next-door neighbor, a really tough job. Having seen thousands of articles in his life, and editing several of them every day, Reductionist had become excellent at categorizing ideas and pieces of writing. It was really difficult, if not impossible, to come up with something that he would call original. This caused fierce competition, and jealousies, among the three writers.

Reductionist often invited his neighbors to accompany him whenever he was invited to a program on writing. Rational especially liked them because he learned new things from different people. Romantic preferred staying alone, but different settings opened fresh paths for new inspirations. Regular, on the other hand, disliked the idea of traveling because it disturbed his daily schedule, but he reasoned it was okay making time for friends, as part of his larger schedule.

At the end of one of those trips, they were traveling back home on a dark and rainy night.

As they covered each mile of the road, they talked about many things. After some random subjects, they started talking about the topic that interested them all: writing. They discussed different issues, such as how to start writing, how to write well, how to make your words carry meanings that would satisfy the mind and the heart, and so on. On the issue of inspiration and new ideas, Romantic told a short story:

"A farmer had two fields. He started cultivating both. After the first season, he saw that one of the lands was yielding produce but the other one didn't. Several consecutive trials only confirmed the quality of the fertile one. The more trials the farmer made, the faster he received the produce and the more he reaped. Then the farmer decided not to use the barren field anymore.

"The inspirations are gifts from God. He plants seeds in our hearts in that way. People who value and pay due respect to inspiration are like the fertile field in the story. The farmer enjoys the produce and uses that field more. People who ignore inspiration or postpone dealing with it are the barren land. They don't foster the seed, and the farmer ceases using them."

After the apt parable, everybody was submerged in silent reverie for a while. Romantic suggested, "Why don't we pull over and talk about this together for peace of mind? I'm really enjoying this." But Rational did not share her perspective. "You know, I really would love to, but we have a long way to go. It is not wise to stop and forget about our trip. What are you going to do when we are all sleepy and not able to continue on the way? And what is wrong with talking while traveling, anyway?"

Romantic started crying. "You never listen to me; you always want me to forget my heart. I feel as if I am among friends who are like dead statues." Irritated by the words of Romantic, Regular tried to manage everyone's feelings. "Hey, I think focusing on the discussion is a good idea, but it is not what we usually do. We are not near a lake or on top of a hill. It is neither sunset nor nighttime in a café. So, it may be better to wait until tomorrow." Although these words were as neutral as they could be, Romantic still felt neglected. "I don't think you will give yourselves over to the matter if we keep going and talking at the same time. Instead, you will exploit and consume this lovely talk as a means to stay awake. This is a clear betrayal; it is hypocrisy toward your heart."

"Wait a minute. I don't think wisdom is the same thing as hypocrisy. Do you have a really good reason to forget about everything else for the sake of this topic? I mean, what makes this topic so important that you want us all to sacrifice everything for it?" rebutted Rational.

Romantic could not answer this question, and turned her face outward into the darkness of the forest. She thought, "I am just like those trees and flowers that suffer from not being able to display their beauty because of the darkness."

Reductionist, who was driving while listening to all the talk, said, "What is it that you are aiming to get from this talk, whether we do it now or later? I don't want to be discouraging, but isn't this merely another hay fire giving a burst of heat and light that will prove ordinary and transient in the end? This is just another emotion-provoking breeze about inspiration. I have experienced several of those, and yet here comes another. What difference is this going to make when we already have thousands of them out there? What is the point in discovering America over and over?"

At this argument, Romantic, Rational and Regular shut their mouths. Although the three roommates wanted to talk about the new perspective that Romantic had presented, their dispute about how to do it had weakened them in the face of Reductionist's arguments. Nobody could say a word after Reductionist had spoken, and silence covered the quartet like the night.

Although she had been upset by the rest of the group, Romantic was still awake and happy in her mind. She decided to daydream about previous inspirations she had received. That way, she relived the exhilaration and joy. Triggered by that energy, Romantic's giggle disrupted the increasing weight of the dark and silence. Rational, sorry to have upset Romantic, used the broken silence as an opportunity: "I have an idea. By going slower, we can sincerely concentrate on each other and on Romantic's inspirations. That way, we can convert our trip into a journey toward the writing of an article." This suggestion triggered Regular to say: "Yes, depressing nights are a regular feature of our in-depth talks." Everybody waited for Reductionist to approve. Reductionist slowed down. The lessened noise from the engine strengthened the silence. In the tense atmosphere, Reductionist laughed like a thunderclap, and said, "I am going to tell you guys a little story. A writer had three pens. He picked the first one and wrote an article with it. After finishing it, the pen said, 'I wrote this article for you. Do you like it?' The writer smiled back and said, 'Yes, thank you.' Then the writer put that pen in his office so that it could do things for him. Another day, the writer used the second pen to write a piece. After he finished it, the pen turned to him and said, 'I wrote what you told me. Do you like it?' The writer smiled back and said, 'Yes, thank you.' Then the writer put that pen in his bag so that it would write things while traveling. And finally the writer used his third pen to write another article. After finishing it, the pen turned to him with a smile and said, 'Thank you for using me.' The writer smiled back at the third pen and placed it in his pocket, next to his heart. He carried it everywhere he went, and whenever he had an original idea, he welcomed it with the help of his third pen."

By that time, the rain outside had turned into a shower of smiles inside the car. Motivated by the unexpected story Reductionist had told, everybody welcomed the inspiration that came from the pen next to the heart. Romantic was not late taking her turn: "You know, for everything there is a season. You have to sow your seeds in the fall and wait until summer to reap. If you sow any time else, you not only waste your time but also lose your seeds. So, I guess the best time to work on an idea is when it first descends from the heavens to your heart."

Both Regular and Rational looked at Romantic with wide-open eyes. Regular said, "You have an important point there."

"That is absolutely right," concluded Rational.

INSPIRING STORY

from the memoirs of an inventor that lived long, long ago

I especially love when spider webs shine with the sunrise. The little water beads on the delicate threads make an extraordinary scene in the early morning dawn. How they make their webs is quite beautiful. It blows my mind that they can weave such long and complex patterns despite their tiny bodies. With the colorful designs on their bodies, spiders are a manifestation of the beauty that penetrates the smallest holes of the earth. Speaking of spiders, I would like to share with you a lovely memory about how my admiration of them led me to the discovery of my life.

In those times, there was not much to do other than hunting and gathering leaves and fruit. I wanted to do something else. The skins of the animals were so perfectly fitting, flexible, warm and nice for them. We tried to wear them ourselves, but they did not fit us. They did not totally cover our bodies, and they smelled terrible. I wanted to come up with a new way of covering our bodies. I sat by the spiders and reflected on this need a lot while watching them make their webs.

Not everyone was appreciative of the spiders and my interest in them. Whenever my father caught me watching the spiders, he mocked and reprimand me for being lazy. He always told me to get going on hunting something edible, in order not to sleep with empty bellies. You can imagine what torture it was for me to hunt. Killing something of beauty is not beautiful. I knew we had to eat to survive. But perhaps I was not the right person to do the killing part. I could cook, I could pick fruit…

One day, when I was watching a spider, I saw a cocoon hanging down from the tree. That was it! The cocoon's cover was what I was looking for: a large spider web woven densely enough to cover us. You should have seen me when the idea first came to my mind. I couldn't help but smile broadly. It had been a long time since I had such a joyous smile. I started running and climbing hills. To rest, I watched the valleys below. Then once again I took off, soaring down from the hill at speed; my arms wide open like a bird's wings.

When I came home, empty-handed to be sure, my mother was not happy at all. "If you don't want your father to ruin your night, go and find something before he comes," she said. Fortunately, I knew some trees that were in fruit just then. I rushed to gather from them to make everybody happy.

Later that night, I had a very scary dream. I was running when I suddenly fell into a pit in which there was a long snake. The snake started to wind itself around me so that I was completely covered. I saw there was a scorpion in the pit, though it could not approach me because of the snake. I woke up screaming. My parents came in to check on me. After a second's silence, my father said, "I told you not to watch those spiders too much."

Although I was not bothered, my parents were getting more and more concerned about me. I was getting to the age of marriage, and they wanted me to have sound spiritual health. The next day, we visited the man of God in our village so he would interpret my dream and give advice. He said, "The snake in your dream did not harm you. It is to be hoped that God will bless you with a cover that is going to protect you from worldly and heavenly harms." This interpretation was unexpected by both me and my parents.

Soon afterward, I talked about my inspiration to my mother, and she told me something invaluable. She said that our great-great-grandparents had worn beautiful things before they came to this world. When they were sent down here, their beautiful clothes were ripped off. Now that I was thinking about making beautiful garments, perhaps this was a heavenly message. My mother wanted me to keep it secret.

I did keep my hopes and inspirations secret, but I did not stop working on them. Then I was inspired by another creature: birds. They made their nests by weaving plants and branches together. That observation brought me to the brink of the discovery of my life, though I did not know it at the time.

One day, my mother wanted to have a private conversation with me. She said that now I was not a girl anymore but a young woman, and it was time that I united my life with someone else. She said that our guests from a few days earlier had come to talk about this; they had asked my parents for me. At first, I was perplexed. I wanted to have some time to prepare myself for the idea. But not long after, the preparations for the wedding were underway, and I was quite willing, because of the person asking for me.

My groom was the man of God who had interpreted my dream. To suit his status, I wanted to wear something special on the day of the wedding, something never before seen. The days ran by too fast, interfering with my inability to come up with that special thing, and I started spending more time alone with the spider webs. My mother thought a gloomy state had befallen me due to my upcoming wedding. She tried to reassure me, to calm me, but that was not what I needed. As my state persisted, my parents' worries grew. They did not want any trouble in my wedding or marriage.

One day, I received the first gift, even before the wedding took place. I was suddenly inspired to weave the leaves and stems of plants to cover myself, like the winding of the snake in my dream, like the cocoon of the spider. Fueled by the joy of this heavenly gift, I quickly finished making my garment. The discovery was surely a heavenly beauty sent to celebrate my marriage. Wearing the new garment, I was so beautiful, and with the love of my life, I was so happy.

BIG GERMINATION

I t was one of those chilly, lively mornings of spring. Everything was as expected. Creeks were flowing, birds were flying, insects were waking up to a new life, and trees in the forest were silently but constantly growing. The ambient noise increased as the sun rose above the mountains.

The morning was unusual for one of the ants, Sayhon. He was intrigued by the noises coming from all directions. He had recorded the noise generated by bugs when carrying chips of wood, the sound a fly makes when landing on a dry leaf, the clamor of the creeks as they hit the rocks, and so on. But within the cacophony of sounds, Sayhon was always able to filter out a background noise that showed up consistently. It was as if something or someone was omnipresent in every occurrence, making itself heard. After this realization, the poor ant secluded himself to concentrate on the subtle message. After a while, not able to figure out the source of this constant noise, nor able to come up with an explanation of its meaning, Sayhon spiraled down into an endless depression. In hard times like these, he always took refuge in the warm friendship of Nurson.

Nurson also conducted his own research, by modeling the dynamic geometry of the forest. Noting variations in the locations of the fruits on the ground or branch, he benefited the worker ants in establishing the optimum routes for collection. Even more challenging was Nurson's interest in predicting the time and place of a new fruit's birth. It was so demanding, this prediction effort, that it shook his antennas wildly. During his research, Nurson had come to the conclusion that, whether old or newborn, all the fruit were moving apart from each other. This effect was more evident in the observation of fruit at large distances.

One day when it was raining, Sayhon observed the raindrops splashing on the water, and how they made a blasting sound. Nearby Nurson was studying the expansion of the waves in the puddles made by raindrops. After some gloomy moments, Sayhon wanted to start a conversation.

"Hey, man! Do you hear any noise generated by those waves?"

"Yes!" yelled Nurson, hysterically.

Sayhon was not expecting such an enthusiastic answer to his question. It rather sounded like an answer to something else. In truth, this was the case. Nurson had had an epiphany from Sayhon's question: The noise you are detecting everywhere is due to the expansion of the forest.

Sayhon was startled by the answer he had received. Nevertheless, he was eager to continue the conversation. "Hey! Easy now, easy."

"Look! The noise you are detecting everywhere points to an entity or occurrence that is omnipresent. To date, we don't know an entity everywhere, but we do know an occurrence that is everywhere: the moving apart phenomenon. So, the only thing that can create this noise you are so curious about is the expansion of the forest. Every fruit and every branch in this forest is moving apart from each other, while leaving behind a signature in the form of sound. Now everything makes sense."

Enlightenment suddenly seized them both, manifested by a shiver throughout their bodies. When they came back to their senses, they couldn't help but smile, and it didn't take long before Sayhon and Nurson began squealing in joy.

Soon, the entire ant colony was in a tumult about the discovery of the expansion of the forest. There were subsequent related thoughts. For example, an ant suggested that the omnipresent noise must be propagating through some unseen but all-pervading substance, but the experiments to verify this suggestion failed. Another discussion revolved around the size of the forest. Some claimed that it was impossible to know the size of the forest, while others said it was finite, since otherwise it would result in an infinitely intertwined forest. A third heated argument was the age of the forest. The expansion theory stated that since the forest is expanding now, rewinding this process long enough means ending up with a single tree, and eventually a single seed, out of which this endless forest has formed. They called this unimaginable start the "big germination." Based on the big germination theory, some ants suggested billions of years for the age of the forest, while others claimed a younger age of thousands based on their interpretation of the ancient texts.

In the fresh vibrations of these findings, the discussions of the ants about the start of the forest eventually became a discussion of their own existence. What was the origin of life in the forest? How had the living beings come to their current states, each with an optimum design for the survival of its own species and for the well-being of the entire ecosystem? Were they merely fallen off a tree as a result of a coincidence?

As the founders of the big germination theory, Sayhon and Nurson were invited to speak in huge assemblies where thousands of curious ants were gathered. They had given several interviews, and participated in many events on the origin of life. The two friends had differing points of views on this matter, but their discussion was as respectful as it was rational.

Sayhon held the view that living beings had come to existence through a chain of events not yet known to the ants, but able to be discovered through advancements in science. As his initial hypothesis, he proposed a common ancestor to all kinds of animals in the forest, like the start of the forest from a single seed. He supported his theory of a common ancestor with the observations of common traits among different organisms. But eventually, he admitted that his hypothesis is only tentative, and needed further scrutiny. He was open to changing his views based on new findings and observations, and never suggested that his hypothesis be used as the criterion to judge the veracity of new perspectives.

Nurson, on the other side, claimed that the origin of life in the forest was by the hand of the Creator, just like He was the one who had created the forest in the scenario of the big germination. In the same context, he thought that the scientific studies must be aimed at learning how the Creator was making different kinds of animals in the forest. Nurson said that his view did not essentially differ from Sayhon's views in terms of scientific foundations or implications, but he positioned himself against unscientific interpretations of scientific findings. For example, as he admitted his belief in the Creator is an unscientific presumption, Sayhon must admit his claims about a common ancestor is unscientific, since there was no absolute proof to it. Nurson also expressed his resentment about the ants who inferred the absence of the Creator in the scientific texts as a rejection of Him, since such inference was clearly irrational as well. Overall, Nurson neither tried to alienate Sayhon nor curse his views, he merely requested that both parties characterize their views properly, which was wholeheartedly approved by Sayhon.

In return to the request of Nurson, Sayhon invited him to admit that they don't have a complete understanding of how creation occurs, and that interpretation of implicit information in the ancient texts cannot be binding. Nurson humbly agreed.

Despite the friendly opposition between Sayhon and Nurson, the ant colony was severely divided into two groups: some siding with Sayhon and others agreeing with Nurson. Each group projected their own view as the ultimate truth, unlike the two friends' own admittance of the unscientific parts in their views. Although Sayhon and Nurson both acknowledged the tentative and immature level of science in the theories, the public preferred to embrace them as complete, unchangeable, incontrovertible truths. These two groups showed intellectual hostility and socially excluded each other. Rejecting the other's views in their entirety, they mutually evolved into antagonists.

Strangely enough, as the tension between these groups increased, the climate in the forest started to change dramatically. Rain became more abundant, yet the weather also warmed up significantly. They had yet to discover the significance of these drastic changes, but this threat to the entire colony acted as a unifying force among the ants, mitigating their divisions on the origin of life.

On one of those hot days, the ants noticed large cracks forming in their nests, which eventually evolved into large channels, through which a violent stream came and flooded the forest. Many of the ants saved themselves by floating on leaves. Now everything was underwater, and would be until it soaked completely into the soil, which was unlikely to occur in their lifetimes. Facing extinction, the big germination and the subsequent expansion of the forest felt like meaningless topics. And yet, the origin of life was of the highest attention. Even the most bigoted ants who denied the Creator wanted to believe in a higher Hand that could penetrate the doom they were facing and deliver them to salvation.

The flood did not return the ants back home but carried them to another one. By the time they arrived at this new forest, the massive flood had dwindled down to a pleasant stream, and the ants could disembark safely from their leaves. With no possessions, everything had to be reconstructed: a home, a safe environment, and most importantly, the hope for restoration.

Sayhon and Nurson were among the survivors. Seeing that their home forest actually had an end had stunned them. In light of this fact, they had to reconsider all their thoughts from scratch. This was not to be done publicly, because the colony was struggling for survival. In this new land of uncertainties, everyone was in need of a truth to cling to, and the suppositions of Sayhon and Nurson were the last thing they looked for.

As the colony's outward efforts for reconstruction and the two ants' inward quests continued, they came across the most unexpected thing: another ant colony like their own. The meeting was as shocking to the native ants as it was to themselves. As their relationship deepened, it was a subtle, mind-altering experience for all of them to see that they both had religious texts telling the same brief story about the origin of life.

HEARING THE LIGHT

One Saturday morning, I was sitting in our neighborhood park. It was especially lovely this time of the year. The birds start chanting after a winter-long silence, flowers spread their mesmerizing scents, and the breezes sing operas of resurrection constantly in my ears. Often, I stop in the middle of my walk to feel the air on my nose, my cheeks. On my ears and in my hair, I feel it with every cell in my body. As I resume walking, I sometimes turn the solo of a flutist cardinal into a duet, or hold my breath while a locust sings its sonata. Indeed, I feel the coming of spring as a yearly renovation in my soul.

It's funny, though. Sometimes while I walk in the enchantment of awakening nature, I run up to a tree, and hug it as if it's a friend. Imagine how entertaining I am to passersby!

It was one such day when I felt the presence of a second person nearby. Strangely enough, though, he wasn't laughing at me hugging the tree.

"Hi there, sport, what is wrong with you? Why aren't you laughing at this lunatic who is in love with trees instead of people?" I asked.

I was shocked to hear his answer: "The sight of people is of no value to me because I cannot see the light coming from them. But you are certainly shining through your voice. For me, people shine through their presence; they change my heartbeat."

To cover my anxiety, I exhaled the air that was hiding in my lungs, and teased, with some bravado: "So, I should be careful when I am talking to you since I cannot hide my true feelings from you!"

"You bet. But don't worry; your voice is giving me positive signals."

I quickly returned: "I am happy to hear that. So, shall we play a game together?"

"Like what?"

"All right. With only listening, we are going to try to predict the coming of the next person."

"I accept your challenge," he said.

We kept silent in order not to miss the clues of an approaching person. Believe it or not, we waited for many minutes and not a single person passed by. We could hear the voices of kids running in the distance, wind rubbing the leaves, the branches of the trees crackling as they sway, flies buzzing, birds flying or landing, but not a single person passing by. Suddenly he said:

"Maybe we should play something else."

"You know what? You are first person with whom I can play the game of solitude. We are together, but not like cans on a shelf. We are together like two flowers smiling at each other although we cannot see or hear one another. Outsiders may think we are lonely. But in essence, we are hand in hand in the depths of our hearts."

"It is strange that you say this. Why should you enjoy solitude?" he asked.

I did not answer. My silence was my answer; I think, or rather hope, he got my answer. I didn't want my discovery of a companion in solitude to disappear so abruptly.

"Here comes one!" he exclaimed. I could feel his joy in catching the first person. I smiled, and he felt it; I give out a warm, vibrating breath when I smile.

"It is so alive," he said.

"What? The person?" I was startled. Why was he using "it" for a person?

"No, your smile. I don't feel many smiles like yours. I usually hear frozen laughs and smiles of mass-production, which carry no sincerity."

I was embarrassed by his compliment. Again I kept silent, but my face was burning up, and he felt that as well.

"Now you are as flushed as I was when we started talking."

"Yes, what had happened to you? Why were you so flushed earlier?" I asked.

"I climb this tree often. I do this whenever there is nice weather. Sometimes I feel the footsteps of someone who I want to catch. I rush down to the ground hoping not to miss the encounter. But always, I miss the person. Now, that spirit is standing before me."

Once more, I was embarrassed. I didn't know what to say. We both kept silent for a while. Then, I heard my daughter calling: "Dad, it's time."

She was the one predicted by my companion in solitude.

"Forgive me for disturbing your conversation," she added.

"A conversation by presence cannot be disturbed by words," replied my friend. We all chuckled.

I felt my daughter pulling my arm, a clear sign meaning "let's go." I grasped her hand firmly, turned back to my companion in solitude, and gave a silent goodbye, which he returned. Then I gave him that lively grin, and he withstood its heat. I picked up my cane and started knocking on his ears again as I returned home with my daughter as my guide.

BEAUTY IN THE SKY

I t was a clear blue sky when I heard a sound that cut through my brain and nailed me in place. I looked where it was coming from, but could not see anything. No matter how I tried to follow it, it constantly escaped my gaze, as if hiding from me. My eyes were frozen in the direction I last heard it.

Not long after, I saw a minuscule thing coming toward me from that direction; I thought it was a bird of some kind. Strangely enough, the bird came to me so abruptly that I heard its sound only after it passed me. Guess what? It was not a bird; it was a fighter jet. This time, I knew where to look, and I followed it while it played peek-a-boo with me.

The following day, my mother took me to the celebration arena for a national holiday. I couldn't believe my eyes. Everywhere there were fighter jets; my eyes sought the one that had mesmerized me the day before. It was parked before me, as if waiting for me to come. I approached it respectfully, and carefully touched it. It was so cold and tough, yet so beautiful. That day, I knew what I wanted to be when I grew up. The smell of the jet fumes was so powerful that I felt I could fly with such a drink.

"Hey, come here!" I heard someone calling me. But there was nobody nearby. "Follow the sharp smell; come over here," the voice insisted. Was I daydreaming? Had I become drunk from the jet fumes and lost my conscience? Indeed, the voice was coming from the rear of the engine. The nozzle was talking to me!

The next moment, I found myself in the circular, hollow structure of the nozzle. I was too astonished and fearful at first, but after looking around admiringly, I spoke: "I have seen the inferno fire that you are exhausting. Isn't it beautiful? You are so powerful. You are the one that is powering this beauty in the sky."

The nozzle was not happy to hear my words of flattery. "Hey, little boy, you may know something, but you don't know everything. Yes, it is true that I am using that violent river of gas. You are right that this stormy exhaust is at the heart of this beauty in the sky. But you must learn more. I am only a solid duct that accelerates what comes into me. I have no power to compress that humongous volume of air into an amount as small as a bird's nest. I am completely unable to heat up the air to inferno levels. And the beauty in the sky is not taken up there by me, either."

I was totally disappointed and frustrated by the nozzle's speech. For an instant I had thought it was my hero; now, my dreams were dashed. I felt alone in a desert. The nozzle must have realized this, so it piped up again: "Come on. I am going to introduce you to the unsung heroes behind our mysterious beauty. I am going to show you the inside."

I was truly perplexed. What could be more mysterious than a speaking nozzle? The voice of the nozzle disappeared into a deep, dark hallway, into the engine, where I followed. I went by long towers with a nicely curved shape. As soon as I stepped near them, the floor at the foot of the towers started moving. In the midst of this earthquake and blinding darkness, I could faintly see another row of towers that were immobile. I threw myself toward them. Deep in my horrified and troubled soul, I heard a thunderous voice that reverberated everywhere:

"How nice to see you here, Adam!" I was doubly shocked. Not only was this unseen thing talking to me, but it also knew my name. "Do you know me?" I asked. "How could I miss your glittering eyes fixed at us whenever we pass over you? I am the turbine, one of the unseen heroes. I am the one that powers the compressors that squeeze the air. I am the one that faces the hot air before it goes into the nozzle."

This was the legendary hero behind the beauty in the sky! I looked at its towers of nobility and its curved surfaces of beauty. As I was losing myself in admiration, I heard the voice again:

"These are the eyes that I have seen every time we passed over you. But I have to tell you something. What you are looking for is not me either, because I cannot create the hot air that energizes everything, including myself. Despite the beauty and power embodied in me, I am not the essence you are looking for."

What could this mean? First the nozzle, now the turbine; every time I am attracted to the source of power, I am then left alone with a sense of deception. Are they mocking my admiration? If so, they don't deserve my admiration; if not, then why do I feel deceived? Is it so wrong to attribute hero status to something?

Lost in my feelings and thoughts, I left the turbine, and went further into the darkness. Not only did I not know where I was, but I also had no means of determining my whereabouts. In total silence and darkness, I sat in what felt like a smooth, vast room. A hot wind started blowing with increasing speed, and a constant noise filled the space. I was alarmed and looked for something to cling to. With the help of lightning that seemed to spark from nowhere, I saw a cavity that looked safe. After a challenging crawl, I was there. Then a second lightning came and everywhere burst into flames. It was as if the winds of hell had been released. My jaw dropped as I stared at this miraculous display of fire.

"Welcome! Finally you are here," said a booming voice, distinct despite the violent storm. I felt as if I was being driven through a scene written down long ago, where I experienced things that I alone was meant to. "Am I the hero of this scenario?" I wondered silently, and laughed at the idea. By seeing so many extraordinary things at once, my instinctive awe was being veiled. I couldn't pay the respect due to the voice I heard. Suddenly I received a kick from behind, and I had to struggle against the fiery winds to get back to my safe and comfortable seat.

"Hello! Are you still there?" I asked. "Can you tell me where I am?" The distinct voice appeared again in my ears: "Indeed, I am here, but you were not!" I bowed my head in shame. Having hurt the only one who could help me in this situation was foolish. "And I was with you all along from the start." What was this? I didn't know whether to feel ashamed because of my self-centered, misplaced respect, or to burst into a thousand pieces for having not recognized the one who was with me all along?

"This is as far as you can go in this story. You are in the place where the energy that empowers everything is revealed. It is the heart of the beauty that you have been admiring." After a second of silence, the voice continued: "Did you find what you were looking for?" I had seen strange things, but none had satisfied my heart or quenched my curiosity. My only answer was a downturned face, though I didn't know if the voice could see my countenance. Apparently it did, for it directed me to another place. "You see this violent fire going on? Would you like to fly away with it?" Was this guy crazy? How in the world could I survive in fire? "There are just two ways to get out of here. Either you fight the fire back to where you came from. Or, if you are not able to do so, you go forward."

With that directive, I started crawling forward, into the strong wind. I came across something similar to the turbine, then another hallway similar to the nozzle. At first I was puzzled, because I was seeing the same things. Had I made a mistake and gone backward? That couldn't be the case, since I had moved away from the fire.

After this stupefying similarity, I was at the mouth of the cave where everything starts. I was able to see the wings. But now, the aircraft was moving. The storm going on inside was for accelerating. The force of the acceleration was so strong that I slipped from where I was clinging, and found myself stuck at the beautiful front curve of the wing. Impossibly, the same voice welcomed me again: "Finally, you are here." I didn't know whether to reply or lose myself in the beauty of the aircraft as it soared into the air with ever-increasing speed. I felt like the ocean divers who hear a beautiful voice when they go deeper than they should. My body could not resist melting in the excitement of the maneuvers. Moments later, we were hundreds of meters above where we had started. Now, the aircraft was cruising, and despite the rarity of the experience, it was as comfortable as sitting in my living room. With the steadiness of my environment, I found myself emerging from the depths of excitement.

"Have you found the beauty you are looking for?" asked the voice again, and I said yes. "Where do you think that beauty is coming from? From the engines or from the wings?" It was a most unexpected question. My mind raced. The engine itself was not able to fly, it was able only to create a strong push. The wings were beautiful, but they did not actively do anything until the lift was there. Without the air, the wings could not balance the aircraft. But air alone completely sinks us. "I don't know where the beauty is coming from. There seems to be something missing in the ingredients that created the beauty of flight. None of the ingredients seems to originate flight It is as if you put the engine, the wings and the air in a pot, and suddenly something that you did not put there comes into being."

"But you did not realize this until you made this journey, though you have been witnessing the same beauty all along."

Why was that the case? Why did I have to make this incredible journey in order to become aware of this uncertainty in the source of flight?

"Perhaps from outside you may take all the mysteries for granted, because you consider them natural, ordinary. But once you are inside, you realize there is something intangible that is not you nor the things you come across. It is as if somebody is tracking what happens, and whenever the necessary ingredients are there, he secretly adds the missing spice in just the right amount. And then? Behold the beauty!"

STORY IN PROGRESS

Every year, 12 to 25 million people attempt suicide worldwide, and 1 million of them achieve what they were aiming to achieve. That means that every 30 seconds, one person is dying by suicide. Be it a child, an elder, or an adult, suicide victims come from all ages.

Fred (not his real name) is 21 years old, living in a university community. Last year, he performed a project to "stretch into infinity" – i.e. he attempted suicide. Fortunately, his project failed. After his return to normal life, he found an alternative way to infinity. I wanted to interview him as soon as I learned about his story, which he accepted.

"I am doing a double major in mathematics and biology. Unlike the regular biology students who are educated to think traditionally and memorize constantly, my way of thinking is rather mathematical and rational."

I wanted to punch a hole in this super confident young boy's claims about himself. "So, you never fell in love, but instead, rationally proved that some girl was the one meant for you?"

He chuckled. "I guess, I did fall in love, but suppressed my feelings since they were irrational."

"Then you must have a strong will. How do you rationally explain the human will? I mean, we are talking about a young man whose hormones are keeping him at the verge of love. And how do you think your will fights against these molecules that pervade your body?"

"My thoughts on this are different now, but at the time, I was trying to express everything in terms of testable, concrete concepts. There is so much research on the effects of genes and the environmental conditions on human behavior. So, my will had to be some proteins synthesized from my DNA."

"So do you think, or did you think, that one day people could use love pills to maintain their

love for their partners, and to have compassion
for their children?"

"Why not? Actually, it is not just that. I
had many thoughts that engulfed my mind and
motivated my actions, including my attempted
suicide. I couldn't receive rationally satisfactory
alternatives to my conclusions."

Then Fred took me on a tour d'horizon of his
view of life and people. There were many elements in his views that you could hear from other
people, but this one was unique and noteworthy:

"This is a bit irrelevant, but I can tell you a
funny one too. If the speeding tickets are issued
not due to actual harm but due to the increased
risk of harm, then people who drink more than a
minimal amount should be given drinking tickets. Statistically speaking, the number of crimes
linked to speeding is nowhere close to the number of crimes linked to drinking. So, if I am getting a ticket for speeding, although I haven't
harmed anyone, then why isn't my friend for
whom I am the designated driver, getting a ticket for his increased potential to harm someone?"

Speechless, I tried to steer him back to his
conclusions that led him to what he did.

"You know, I was never hospitalized for depression. Nobody thought that I was in deep trouble, including me. I was considered to be an intellectual, an extraordinary friend. I don't know how it goes with other people, but when the idea came, it wasn't like a freaky idea to entertain myself for a minute. It came as an irrefutable theory. It only made sense. Really."

The idea of suicide making sense? That didn't make sense to me! Seeing my blurred gaze, he continued.

"If motivation is essential to accomplish your ideals, how could something that brings motivation be considered harmful?"

He was talking about drugs.

"If success is all about hard work, then why is it forbidden to pave your way to success rather than leave it to luck?"

That is, fortifying hard work through taking drugs.

"If my mental activity is nothing but complex dynamics of molecules in my brain, then shouldn't I take drugs that are the embodiment of rejuvenating and exhilarating inspirations leading to innovations?"

After a slight pause, he concluded:

"If happiness is all about certain molecules in my body, then what is wrong about getting it directly rather than mining it through thorny relationships with people?"

How would you answer these questions, knowing that they are asked by an individual in the making who is trying to make sense of life but who is bewildered by the discrepancies within mature people?

"My line of thought and other people's line of thought in this matter are similar to the graph of $1/x$. We are both aiming for the same point, i.e. zero. But our distinct approaches take us in opposite directions. The two couldn't be more divergent than this."

In mathematical elegance, Fred was describing the state that nurtured his suicidal thoughts. He could not establish ties with the rest of us. With an intention to never come back, Fred used drugs to become a zero in our world, and to stretch into an unknown infinity. Did he succeed?

"But you know, like a sad love story, $1/x$ never converges to zero. I failed, too, in that sense. The way I conceived it, death was going to be a culmination of motivation, success, and happiness. I aimed for it head on. According to my conviction, I was supposed to have achieved all of those. When I opened my eyes in the hospital, I realized that I had neither success nor happiness."

You don't have to be a sage in order to understand that suicide is not a key to success or happiness. But a brief journey to death made Fred a sage.

"It is possible in this life that one receives death while perfectly healthy. It is also possible that one can survive despite miserable health. In other words, just like being healthy doesn't necessarily mean you can't die, there isn't a mechanic relationship between being unhealthy and arriving at death. My own failure to die despite what happened to me is living proof of this."

I noted in my mind that this was a good example of learning from your failures.

"The moment I realized that death is given, just like life is, my suicide attempt transformed from being a story of failure to a story of success, because that's when I started believing in the unseen."

Believing in the unseen was a quality that Fred did not have before, but why and how had it been the elixir that changed his failure into success?

"It is so ironic and controversial. In the beginning, what I was missing was my acceptance of self-deficiency in grasping existence. In the end, by admitting to be incomplete, I was becoming complete; being completed by God."

Suicide is one of the most severe sins one can commit, according to monotheistic religions. Yet, this young man found God in the very sin that could throw him light years away from God.

"I don't define myself anymore as an outstanding, perfect intellectual as my friends used to call me. Instead, I am a story in progress. No matter how severe the calamities or how satisfying the joys are, I don't come to an end unless my author ends the story."

... and a Rock Falls

I am watching a little tree, illuminated by sunlight, pushing its way up through the other grown, adult trees. Next to the rustling of the leaves, I hear the sporadic whizzing of cars. The valley and its dry streambed accompany me. I wish I were closer to the river down the hill. Then I could see varieties of fish and birds, and drink water whenever I want. But I am okay with where I am. I sit under the sun, watching this beautiful view, releasing myself from lifelong burdens.

One sunny day I had a guest. He was quite a generous young man. First he served his blood to the mosquitoes. Considering all the things humans pick from nature, their blood is the fruit that nature can pick in return, right? I call this guest generous because he did not kill the mosquitoes while they sucked his blood. He sat near me, and started pondering the nice valley below. I didn't know at first whether I should talk to him. The snail creeping on me preferred to keep silent, so I decided not to speak.

Soon after, the young man's friend arrived. They started talking about finding water. I thought, "How do you think water can be found at this height of the hill?" But they started digging with their special equipment. I had heard about such things when a group of students had come on a field trip. They had talked about the different kinds of rocks and the minerals in them, their formation in the depths of the earth or under deep water, and how one could find in-valuable fluids by digging through them. Seeing these two young men, I better understood what they had meant.

After a few hours of loud noise, I felt wetness touching me from below. The water was indeed rising in the well the two young men had made, and soon they were shouting with joy. As they celebrated, I was engulfed by an uncomfortable feeling I had when they arrived. After all, this was my place, and they had invaded it.

As if the invasion wasn't enough, the first man stepped on me and spread a cloth. I was enraged at the thought of this man celebrating his victory over me. But then my rage faltered as I watched him. He offered thanks and be-gan to pray. At that moment a sense of warmth spread between us, and I began talking to him every time he came. During his visits, he drank fresh water, sat on me looking at the valley, and delved into his reflections and prayers. I thanked God for giving me a flat surface where someone could pray. Our relationship became so special that when he was not around, I prayed for his return.

Years passed by. Things didn't change much with me, but the man changed a lot. His once-smooth face now looked like the wavy ocean surface. His body was bent like trees on steep hills. Things changed incredibly fast for humans! I felt pity for this man who was troubled by his daily affairs. I prayed that I could be closer to him, to help relieve his pain. My prayers were accepted and this respectable man spent more and more time on me. Sometimes lying, sometimes sitting, but always contemplating or praying.

Sometimes, he brought his grandchildren. These kids did not enjoy being here as much as he. They kept looking at the glasses in their hands that entertained them. Occasionally, they had funny talks with their grandfather. One time they talked about putting stones in the water or burying them in the soil so that they could grow like plants. When I heard those words, I thought about my genesis through the ocean beds and the inferno compartments in the earth. My entire life story was worded so naively and elegantly in the mouths of those children. It is curious how little ones can say complex things so easily.

Those times of amusement made me think about myself. I was a mature rock, and I wanted to have youngsters around me. I prayed to have little ones eager to "rock and roll." Perhaps they would take longer than the humans, maybe they would not be as rambunctious. But I kept praying to have them around.

My prayers were answered sooner than I thought, and I started seeing tiny pebbles parting from me. In my maturity, I had the blessing of giving birth to children all around me. Now, whenever the old man came with his grandchildren, they played with mine, and that gave me immense pleasure.

One day, I saw a group of people with a wooden box on their shoulders. Indeed, it was my friend, brought to meet his Lord. He was buried in the cemetery at the peak of the hill.

It's not easy to lose someone you love. It feels like burying a part of your heart before you actually die. I cried a lot, and I still do, silently, in my own way. I don't want my sorrow to assume the form of a complaint against the decree of our Lord. Yet, I cry nonetheless. Perhaps this grief is what made me so weak. I feel that my end is near, too. The increasing number of little ones all around makes this message impossible to ignore. And yet, I am developing a hope of continuity, because the water springing underneath me penetrates my pores, and water means life.

But the peace that comes with this hope is always followed by the grief of losing my friend, and I cry all my water away. To quench my sorrow, God sent me lots of people. They are everywhere, now that my tears are making a beautiful waterfall. But I miss my friend. I would rather have his prayers than these strangers who laugh with negligence at my sorrow. "Oh my Lord, my friend in the heavens... Oh my Lord, my friend in the heavens..."

REMEMBERING THE SUPER VICTIM

a letter from a villain's mom to a superhero

My husband was never a family man; he was always focused and devoted to his work. To him, a successful business meant power and family was only a minor obligation. Many times, I felt like a burden to my husband. I even began to wonder why we got married in the first place. I wondered how such a workaholic could ever have been romantic.

But it is not my husband, but rather my son, who I want to talk about now. Yesterday was the anniversary of my son's death. It is probably in vain to talk about the last days of his life, because people already know that story. He was part of an incredible story. Unfortunately, he was on the wrong side.

My son learned at an early age how to be like his father, devoted to his work and driven by success. His father did not spend much of his time with us, but when he did, he spent most of the time talking about his successes and the growing influence of his business. It was easy to see that my son was captivated by his father's success. To him, his father was an angel who descended from heaven to tell him stories of miracles and wonders.

My son developed an obsessive interest in machines. From a very young age, he dissembled and re-assembled all sorts of machines and even combined different objects to make his own primitive inventions. Before he went to elementary school, he invented an automated knife that spread butter on his bread, and a pulley that would bring him the remote control. I often found myself pondering my son's future education, wondering what this child could possibly learn at school.

The first week of school, my worries came true when my son was diagnosed with Attention Deficit Hyperactive Disorder (ADHD), and quickly became an outcast. My divorce from his father the same year only made things worse. I didn't know what to do. Although it was not ideal, I still thought it was best for my son to continue to study at a normal public school.

In his second year, a fan club was formed to celebrate the superheroes that made this planet a better place to live. Mr. Incredible, Elastigirl, Frozone, Gazerbeam, Superman, and more, were all invited to this club's biweekly activities. My son, having grown up with the example of his successful father, soon developed an interest in this club. There, my son found an excellent replacement for his father, whom he had missed deeply since our divorce.

One day he returned from the club's activities and was not the same person. I hardly recognized him. The angry-looking, hyperactive outcast was gone, and in his place was a child who was destined to follow his dreams. During dinner, I asked how his day had been. He talked about a man that I "better marry," because he wanted him as his father. Guess who it was: Mr. Incredible.

"I asked and he said he was single and he loved children," my son insisted.

"But I've never met him!" I replied, smiling.

"I'm sure you'll love him," he said.

I was so happy that, after two years of misery and distress, we could have a dinner like mother and son.

The dream went on for a few months, until one night when he came home from a friend's house looking very distraught. I thought perhaps he had a fight with his friend, but it wasn't that. He had tried to tag along with Mr. Incredible but had been kicked out of his car, because Mr. Incredible found him too young and didn't want a sidekick. After all, Mr. Incredible always worked alone. Eventually, my son accepted the situation and realized that he was too young. But his awe of Mr. Incredible never faded. He kept seeking ways to get Mr. Incredible to accept him.

By the time my son was in middle school, companies began to purchase his inventions. He was well on his way to becoming as successful as his father had been. I frequently asked myself what this boy would accomplish in the future. He had already achieved what most people never would in a lifetime. Flying boots were his latest invention. He thought they would capture

Mr. Incredible's attention because flying would greatly improve his ability to fight crime.

Then one night, my son was brought home by the police. I started shaking in astonishment. Had he done something horrible with one of his crazy inventions? It turned out he had tried to help Mr. Incredible at the scene of a robbery, but everything had gone wrong, and Mr. Incredible definitively rejected him as a sidekick. Being an adolescent undergoing puberty, he could not face this latest rejection from his hero. He not only craved acceptance and appreciation, he needed them. After that day, all the Mr. Incredible posters, stickers, and T-shirts were gone from our house. My son started putting up posters of villains, and he started to idolize them.

I couldn't tell anyone, but I was terrified when I found a paper in his room that said, "Revenge of the Bad Guys." I hoped it was a phase, an adolescent fury that would fade in time. And it did, or so I thought.

After he completed his university degree, my son started a company that focused on the research and development of defense systems. With his genius, he achieved immediate success and purchased two islands in the Pacific: one as a home to live with his fiancée and the other as his base of operations. I was a happy mother because after so many years of hard work and worries, I thought my son had finally overcome his difficulties and was moving on with his life.

My dream did not last long. After the government grounded all the superhero activities due to growing public unrest towards them, my son started popularizing his inventions that mimicked the superheroes' abilities: flying boots, a shape-shifter that worked by freezing the humidity in the air, a never-ending rope that never broke, and more. It never occurred to me that this was a disguise to hide his true aim: discovering Mr. Incredible's secret identity and getting revenge for himself and others whose loved ones were injured or killed by the superheroes. I only found out later when one of his journals was given to the police by his fiancée.

You know the rest of the story. My son was struck by a car thrown by Mr. Incredible, killed by the very engine he had invented and built. Mr. Incredible had once been my son's hero, and was now his murderer. What can I say? Congratulations, Mr. Incredible, on another job well done? I hope you can enjoy dinner with your family tonight as I'm writing these lines in unending sorrow.

RADIATION

I am the only survivor from quadruplets. One of my sisters survived only 108 minutes after birth. The death of the second one followed about a half hour later. I spent my childhood with my only remaining sister. Our mother was not there either, because she had died while giving birth to us.

As we were growing into adolescence, I shared many secrets with my sister, be they adventurous or romantic. She was a sister, a close friend, and sometimes a mom. When she died in her flourishing age, I not only lost my third sister but also lost a mom for the second time.

Since then, without distinguishing between friend or foe, I let people approach me. I show affinity to them so that I am considered very sociable. When they start enjoying the beauties of my personality, I am stressed by my need for privacy and security. I easily push everyone away by intimidating them with the very beauties they were attracted to.

So, life has been a bottomless solitude for me … Yes, being alone is part of being noble, and I need my privacy in my ivory tower. But I'd rather not have impenetrable walls between me and people.

What a discrepancy! I have a habit of intimidating people to push them away, but I am complaining of an endless solitude at the same time … Why am I like this? It feels as if there is an unknown person in me, over which I have no control, who is doing things using my body. Should I cry for help? I am stolen!

I thought about this a lot. Was it a psychological inheritance I received from the family? You know that my mother died when giving birth to me and that my sisters followed her. My grandmother also died when giving birth to my mother, and my grand-grandmother died when giving birth to my grandmother. I don't know if it is this strangeness that makes me instinctively seek solitude, so much so that my husband could not stand me. I told him that our relationship could only survive in the polar cold, and he said he can deal with cold but not in a place where there is no one else. Eventually, our marriage ended, after which I realized that I was pregnant.

But life goes on, you know, whether you are a noble who pathetically seeks solitude, or if your mother died when giving birth to you, or if you are a pregnant mom left alone … "The great gears of life turn with irresistible momentum. You either keep pace with them, or get smashed in them." That's what my mother said in her letter to me. And that letter is all I have of her. Though, however much I would like her to be with me, and share my joys of success and sorrows of failure. Maybe she would reveal precious life lessons to me, or whisper her secrets into my ear. Maybe she would reprimand me sometimes … Not a single moment lived with her, not even a smack! I wished that this will not be the lot of my baby, but how?

I thought of Prophet Abraham's wife, Hagar. Alarmed by her baby's cries, she had rushed between two distant hills in search of help. God had replied to her efforts by creating a spring in the middle of the desert, just near her, and guiding travelers there.

Following Hagar's example, I tried taking refuge near people so that my baby would not be in a lonely world. In order not to disturb them, I chose their least used places. But people cast me out of there, lest I contract some illness. I tried fancy yellow dresses to make myself look friendly. But, instead of becoming friends, they put me in glass chambers. I tried to help people with some of their diseases, but except a few, they shunned me since I was too risky to be adopted into medical practice.

Oh my God, despite all my efforts, my baby was going to come into a solitary world like her mom's. I knew I was going to be alone when giving birth, and so was my baby. There was a sour smile on my face every time I thought of her...

But maybe ... Maybe one day, God would guide travelers here, and she could join them, and prosper wherever she ends up. Maybe she could have a stable family, and become the mother of many. And I hope, even in her well-established state, she could still keep her lineage at heart, from our grandest grandmother all the way down to her mother: Uranium, Thorium, Radium, and, me, Radon.

What could I do to make sure that my daughter holds on to her past? Could I write a letter, just like my mother left me? Maybe that was a good option, since I inherited from my mother all the letters left from mother to daughter starting with the grandma, Uranium. Yes, I could abide by the tradition of letters, and tell my daughter how much I loved her even before I could hold her in my arms. I could tell her that she had appeared in my dark night like a bright star, although she was yet in my womb. Maybe this way, she could feel at ease when with people, unlike her mother. She could make real friends and be happy with them, even if I won't see her once.

Yes, I won't see you, sweetie. It is what the doctors told while giving me your glad tidings: that I had cancer, and that my body would not sustain a birth. I had to choose between carrying you and a life without you. I chose to live with you, my precious, even if that meant the end of my life when yours blossomed. When you are going to be reading this letter, I'll be watching you with your aunts. Shine and make us smile with your beauty.

Love,

Your mom Radon

* * *

Radon is one of the noble gases in the periodic table. It is the heaviest, naturally occurring one among them. Due to its size, it is the most likely to establish compounds with other elements, compared to the other noble gases. However, its radioactivity easily breaks the bonds that are established between Radon and other elements. Thus, Radon has very few known compounds.

Radon forms in the radioactive decay chain of Uranium. In this chain, the following elements are formed in order: Uranium, Thorium, Radium, and finally Radon. Radon continues to decay, forming Polonium.

The half-life of Radon changes depending on the isotope at hand. Four known half-lives belonging to different isotopes of Radon are 1.8 hours, 2.4 hours, 14.6 hours, and 92 hours. Radon condenses to form a solid that glows with yellow light due to its radioactivity.

Radon naturally occurs underground, and does not dissolve much in water or other liquids there. When it leaks above surface in the form of gas, it tends to accumulate in the not-well-ventilated parts of the houses, e.g. basements. Exposure to Radon gas is linked with cancer, and so it is considered a health hazard. On the other side, the hot springs that contain trace amounts of Radon gas are used rarely to cure heart disease.

BUTTERFLY EFFECT

You built the cocoon as your sanctuary
To find your new self in tranquility
As you changed, the sanctuary became the enemy
Demolishing your home would be your first duty

Don't worry, you will be okay
You didn't belong there anyway
Embrace life, or else you will be cast away
Remember, you only have a single day

You are now like a newborn star in dreams
Behold your beauty and elegant limbs
Feel the air flow by you, flip your wings
Taste the drops of life on the leaves

I wish I were you, just like a baby
My smiles could buy the world's sympathy
And my cries, they would enslave everybody
Each day, sailing toward a new discovery

But, for what are you still searching in pain?
Don't tell me all this splendor is in vain
You are a blossom in the air, don't be insane
I cannot reason away your ceaseless disdain

Oh butterfly, you have woken me up
Is this face mine or is it makeup
Or am I you in my dream? Reality is messed up
After a life-long delusion, I need a clean up

I am now seeking a beauty
One that I saw in a dream I don't remember
From one flower to another, alas I cannot find it
I am starving, how am I going to survive?

But my yearning for the beauty becomes my food
A beauty whose absence is so powerful,
I cannot even imagine reunion with it,
A beauty that is with me though I am far from it.

BONDING

Once upon a time, a king had a beautiful daughter. She had long, light blue hair, which was cared for, every day, by her maids. Anyone who gazed into her blue eyes was mesmerized – it was like they'd been drawn into the ocean. Being with her would lift the troubles of life, much like flying. Her name was Oxygen.

As Oxygen grew into the age of marriage, all of the young man in the kingdom found themselves in a race to marry her. Every day, she was approached by someone who wanted to display their skills and tricks. At first, it was exciting for Oxygen. But seeing one of those suitors every single day eventually felt like an intruder picking on her door. She started rejecting even just seeing someone. If she was forced to do so, she would reveal her violent face. Seeing her anger, instead of her beauty, would burn the hearts of the suitors.

One day, an unexpected young man appeared around the palace. He was one of the ordinary men, with no outstanding skills or talents. He was the stone master, the lonely young man who would barely talk to anyone. Given his lack of skills and social status, it was not befitting for him to even be close to her Highness. He knew this. So, he was not supposed to be walking near the palace, either; and he knew that, too.

Unfortunately, the guards knew that, too. Only a few moments after he started pacing around, he heard his name being called: "Hey Silicon! Get away from here."

Poor Silicon! He had heard about the beauty of Princess Oxygen, and had listened to stories of her misery. Unlike others whose hearts were burning from the violence of Oxygen, Silicon's heart was burning because he couldn't help her. He was pitiful for her, as much as he himself was in need of pity. That's why he'd had the courage to approach the palace, although he knew what would happen to him.

"Hey, do you hear me! Silicon, get away from here, or else!"

This was the second warning. Had he waited for a third one, it would not be a mere warning but … But he continued, as if he did not hear anything. He didn't have anything to lose, anyway. His head fallen on his chest, his hands tied at his back, he ventured toward the likely places where he could breathe the same air as Oxygen, maybe hear her voice or even see her.

He had gone through this scenario countless times in his mind, and every time he had asked himself, "What are you going to do if she looks at you?" That question was never answered. That's why he was here, in a sense: to figure out the answer. But he could not predict what would happen first: getting caught by Princess Oxygen, or getting arrested by the guards.

Silicon realized that he was going through this scenario without paying much attention to his whereabouts. Perhaps, somewhere close to … the guards: "You have been warned! And now you are under …"

"My protection," came an unexpected voice.

"Your Highness! This man is violating your privacy, and needs to be taught how to be respectful."

"I don't see how anyone can violate my privacy when he is walking in a public place; especially if that someone is going to make a separate palace for me out of the most precious jewels."

Princess Oxygen's words were perplexing both to the guards and to Silicon. He didn't know what to say. First, he was surprised by the protection she gave him, then he was shocked to hear the challenge he was made to accept. However, his odd situation here would not tolerate any objection or questioning.

"You are Silicon, right?"

Silicon had never thought about this moment: an unrehearsed, unpredicted revelation. His name had just been pronounced by the legendary Blue Beauty. He simply nodded.

"I would like to see you tomorrow. I want to go over the details of my palace with you. Also, there is a verse I would like engraved on the walls, which I'll provide later."

Silicon couldn't believe all this was happening. His half-faded mind did not wake up until the following day. But what could be more convincing than him walking past the guards, and them not doing anything as he entered the palace? Yes, it was happening.

Of course, the king had heard about what had happened the previous day. As much as he was surprised by his daughter's decision for a separate palace, he was concerned about her special attention to an ordinary man. It was a delicate situation for the king.

Despite all the odds and nerves, the meeting at the palace went very well, except for Silicon. Princess Oxygen had requested him to adorn this new palace with something that was both existent and non-existent. That kind of thing would not exist even in the weirdest tale. How could Silicon find it?

For days following the meeting, Silicon could not lay a single brick for the construction of this unique palace. Instead, he thought about how to find that matchless thing or who to ask about it. Perhaps someone whose status in society was between existence and non-existence would have an idea ...

He thought about the ascetic who lived in a deep cave at the base of a nearby mountain. This was none other than Carbon.

Silicon had heard a lot about Carbon. Actually, Carbon was one of his heroes when it came to helping people. Almost anywhere Silicon worked, people would tell stories of the past, when Carbon did a favor for them. If Carbon helped so many people in so many different ways, why would he not give a hand to Silicon?

As Silicon entered Carbon's cave, sunlight continuously faded. Eventually, there was no light at all. Who could live in this kind of an environment? "Carbon must be a strange character," Silicon thought. When he was not able to move anymore due to lack of light, Silicon started calling Carbon's name, so that he could hear him, and come to meet.

"Why are you shouting so loud, when I am so close to you?" came a soft voice from unexpectedly nearby. They walked together back to the mouth of the cave.

After an initial greeting, Silicon introduced himself to Carbon, and told why he had come. "In short, I need your wisdom about something

that is both existent and non-existent" concluded Silicon.

"What's going to happen after I tell you what
you need?"

"I am going to head back to the town, and
won't bother you again."

Carbon just nodded while exhaling deeply. Inside, though, he was thinking if this direct answer
was a sign of lack of loyalty or crude honesty. He
bowed his head, and stayed silent for a couple of
seconds. "And what do you think Princess Oxygen is going to do after you build that palace and
adorn it with something that is both existent and
non-existent?"

"I don't know."

"What would you like her to do?"

An irresistible smile covered Silicon's face. "I
guess I would like something impossible to happen."

Carbon looked at Silicon in the eyes, and
continued: "What if, instead of what you would
like her to do, she lets you go and doesn't bother
you again?"

That would actually bother Silicon. He did
not answer this question; just kept silent. Then
Carbon picked up again:

"You had told me that the only thing you wanted was her happiness! If she is happy with that palace, why aren't you?"

At first, Silicon was sad and nervous about getting exposed in his heart. But then, his state transformed to a mild anger: "Carbon, are you going to help me or not? I told you how much of a burden I am under. If you know what I need, just tell me! And, I'll be on my way."

Carbon knew the answer, but he thought Silicon needed more than that to be a confidant for Princess Oxygen.

"I want to help you, but I don't know how I can …"

"Carbon, you helped people in so many unbelievable ways. I am not asking a big favor from you. If you know the answer to my question, just tell me. I don't want anything else. Why is it so difficult to answer a question, if you know the answer?"

With that, Carbon dived into a silence that tortured Silicon. The two stayed calm there until the stars came out. Convinced that Carbon was not going to help him, Silicon set back on the way to the town. He was truly disappointed with Carbon. He was his only hope for figuring out what Oxygen had asked of him. Now, Silicon was on his own. Maybe it was better for him to go to Princess Oxygen, confess his failure, and submit to whatever consequences might follow. After all, he was mere a stone master. But what was going to happen to his love and compassion for Princess Oxygen? And, what about Oxygen's dreams not coming true; wouldn't she be dismayed?

As Silicon was taking reluctant steps down the hill overlooking his town, he started going over the scenario of meeting the princess. What could he say? "I want to please you, but I don't know how I can ..." Would his inability be interpreted as disrespect or, worse, as a lack of love? The opportunity that so many outstanding people could not grasp was in Silicon's hands, and now it was slipping away. What was this thing that is both existent and non-existent at the same time?

Silicon's steps slowed down as his mind created images of disappointment and failure. When he finally arrived at his house, he was happy that no one had seen him. He wanted the night not to end so that he wouldn't have to wake up to the next day. But the night wanted him to sleep …

After Silicon had taken off, Carbon sat there, watching him disappear in the distance. Was it proper that he did not tell Silicon what he knew? This was the first time they had met. Until now, Carbon had vaguely seen Silicon when he was a child, and Silicon had no idea of Carbon other than the stories about him. But now, they had seen each other first hand, and it was not a good "first time"!

Long ago, before Carbon was secluded in this cave, he was actually everywhere in the town. Any time someone needed something, he would appear right there. The four chambers of his heart were like four guest rooms. He would do anything he could to make others happy. Many times, though, after helping others and spending time with them, he would feel his need for solitude, and would go upstairs to the two lobes of his brain. If anybody happened to come to thank him during this time, he would pretend to be absent. Appreciations made him shy, anyway.

After years of serving others and shuttling between his brain and heart, Carbon had realized that everybody was pretty much in good shape, and there was not much need for him anymore. He was bored of doing the same things, anyway. Day by day, Carbon felt less and less a part of the community. Eventually, an unquenchable thirst for renewal and beauty engulfed his soul. He decided to go up to the mountains for an extended seclusion to contemplate and pray.

One day during his time there, Carbon had an enlightening experience. This experience changed him inside out: his feelings, his thoughts, even his body. Carbon realized that this grant was an answer to his prayers for renewal and beauty. For a few days, he only enjoyed his new self by rediscovering his own life and the world in general. Then he started thinking about his return to people.

But for this return, Carbon had two major problems, though: when to return and how to return. He did not want to ruin what he was granted by immaturely exposing it to others' eyes. In other words, he did not want his return to people to become his return to his old self. That would be disrespect to the One who had given him this new body. Silicon's visit to the cave had occurred right in the middle of this spiritual uncertainty, and his departure with frustration only added to Carbon's confusion about himself.

"Silicon is just an innocent young man asking for help" he thought. Carbon had not treated him with adversity, but he had not paid him the due respect, either. Maybe Silicon's coming was a sign from God that it was time for Carbon to return. After all, how could he learn the balance he has been looking for without trying? Carbon realized that by refusing to help Silicon, he had lost the opportunity that had come to his feet … He raised his eyes to the sky. His tears waited a while in his eyes, so as to not disturb the prayers. But the tears were too shy to wait in his eyes, and they fell silently over his cheeks.

The next morning in town, Silicon went to the palace in order to confess his failure. At the gate, he looked at the guards for a second. This was probably the last time he was walking by them to see Princess Oxygen. Having waited for his return, the guards asked in wonder:

"Where have you been? Everyone is asking about you!"

"I went to Carbon to see if he has any idea of the thing that Princess asked for. But he did not tell me anything, although he knew it."

"Are you sure it was him? That doesn't sound like Carbon!"

"How can I mistake that glorious shine of wisdom among dark stones? I am a stone master."

"Glorious shine? That doesn't sound like Carbon, either. He is actually a dark stone. You met someone else young man. Had it been Carbon, he would make your face shine with happiness."

Silicon needed to believe what the guards were telling him, and he actually set back on the way to the mountain where Carbon lived. He quickly went over the hills, and climbed to Carbon's cave. This was exactly it. But, he was again met by that glorious shine, not a dark stone – only this time, he was greeted with a big smile and open arms. Silicon was perplexed by what was going on, but he took it as a good sign.

"The guards at the palace told me that you were actually a dark stone, that you would only make my face shine with happiness!?"

"I was a dark stone who did his best to make others happy. But then, I was entrusted with a secret, which changed me inside out. You requested that secret from me. I didn't know whether to reveal the secret ... nor did I know if you were trustworthy enough to hear it."

After a hesitant wait, Silicon asked "Am I?" If Carbon didn't find him trustworthy enough, Silicon wouldn't get what he needed to make Princess Oxygen happy. Worse, he would learn that he was found not trustworthy enough. But Silicon had no other choice. He had to submit to Carbon's judgment.

Carbon was aware of how vulnerable Silicon was at that instant, much like he was aware of his responsibility to protect but also to spread the secret.

"I am going to tell you the secret. If you are trustworthy, this secret is going to take root in your heart, and will spread into your life. If you are not trustworthy, the secret is going to abandon your memory."

It all sounded so simple, yet so heavy. So easy to venture, so bitter so lose ... But if Carbon was telling him this, he must have been ready to deliver the secret.

"I ask from my Lord that I am going to be a fertile ground for the secret," whispered Silicon.

"Know that existence is all about love. But love itself is not the ultimate quality in life, because love is possessive and invasive. A love that knows when to be there and when to leave alone is the existence that knows how to be non-existent."

While digesting this secret, it didn't take Silicon long to figure out that Oxygen had asked from him to adorn the new palace with his love; an educated love. But how did she know this secret?

"She didn't," said Carbon. "She needed it, and she was guided by her need. Much like you were guided by your need; much like I was guided by my need."

After this talk, Silicon returned to the town, and quickly built a palace out of most precious jewels. As told by Princess Oxygen, the walls of the palace read: "So that your Lord's works are manifest on them." After completion, Silicon proposed to Princess Oxygen. Carbon was present in their wedding with his glorious shine, which had never been seen before. His return was interpreted as a sign that this marriage would be a blessed one. Oxygen and Silicon had beautiful children. Their closest friend, Carbon, named them: Quartz, Opal, Granite, and Sand. When they grew, the kids called him "Uncle Diamond." Silicon never forgot the secret. He regularly spared time to contemplate in solitude on "knowing when to be there and when to leave alone, when to be in the guest rooms and when to take refuge in his mind."

* * *

Oxygen is the most abundant element in the earth's crust, and it is what makes earth the beautiful, blue planet as seen from space. Oxygen is one of the elements with the most electronegativity. It is also a strong oxidizing agent, which in daily life is associated with burning and combustion.

After oxygen, silicon is the second most abundant element in the earth's crust. Materials like clay, cement, porcelain, and sand are all made of silicon. Silicon dioxide is the compound that has both silicon and oxygen in it, and its various crystalline forms make different stones such as granite, sandstone, quartz, and opal. Glass is also made of silicon dioxide. One unique property of silicon is that in its extremely purified state, it is used as a semiconductor, i.e. conducting certain voltages and not conducting others, which is essential in computer technology.

Carbon is the element that marks the existence of life as we know it, hence the name organic compounds. It is present in allotropic variations (diamond, graphite, graphene, etc.), each having different physical and chemical properties. For example, although carbon's other forms are opaque, a diamond is translucent. Due to its wide range of chemical and physical properties, carbon is one of the most useful elements in modern industry. Fossil fuels (petroleum, natural gas, coal) are all carbon based, too. Carbon has six electrons orbiting its nucleus. Carbon's ability to make bonds in so many different ways with so many different elements is enabled by its four valence electrons. The remaining two electrons of Carbon are in the inner energy level and don't come into the picture during the bonding process.

WHY IS GOD INVISIBLE?

Having an adolescent at home is a challenge, but answering their questions without triggering other question is a totally different one. And I should know this, because what else can you expect from the curious daughter of a researcher-father? Almost every day, she unloads a question on me, and the rest of my day is buried into deep thoughts over the answer.

Well, this time, I thought her question was an easy one. She asked, "Dad, why is God invisible?" Wow, that was easy. I felt like a child who knows the answer to the question the teacher asked:

"Our eyes are not capable of seeing Him. There are other things, too, that are invisible for us; like love or intelligence." That was it. I was smiling in celebration of my effortless success. But my daughter, she wasn't smiling: "I didn't ask why we can't see Him. I said why is He invisible; that is why did He choose to be invisible to us?"

Good grief! How in the world should I know? I just tried to save the moment by giving the most straight forward answer: "Well, this life is an examination for humans. God invites us to find Him, and choose to submit to Him without seeing. That's the rule of the game, or the challenge of the exam."

She didn't look satisfied with what I said. After a few seconds of silence, she blurted out: "OK, it is part of what I am looking for, but not exactly."

"If you can define what you are after, we can search for it, you know."

"Dad! I remember you telling me that you can ask the perfect question only if, and when, you know the answer. If I don't know the answer, how can I perfectly ask about it?"

Right there, I was shot with my own gun. I had used those words a few times to escape a mental fight or to avoid getting caught with an insufficient explanation. But, being daddy's girl, she picked it up too quickly and she was expecting me to figure out what in her mind without her telling me. So this was something I was used to. All I needed was to focus: "Why is God invisible? Why did He choose to be invisible?"

Being invisible while being there... Things are better understood when juxtaposed with their opposites. So, I started thinking about being visible but not being there. This sounded like the people who shake hands with you while talking to somebody else, or those who can't help looking at a computer or cell phone screen while talking with you. Then I remembered the cliché father depiction in the movies: a person who exists but no more—and the rest of the movie is focused on filling that void from lack of a father's love! I realized that my brainstorm was taking me far away... But the concept of parenthood? Maybe there was help in it.

Being good parents... I recalled the examples in the books and seminars about parenting. "Helicopter" parents would help their child in everything to the point that they would not let the child enjoy the feeling of success. Such kids would have difficulty in developing self-confidence and entrepreneurship. "Absentee parents," on the other hand, would not bother themselves, even if their kids were crushed under incessant failure. Such kids would have difficulty in developing trust and establishing long-term commitment. But what about these musings? Were they of help to probe into my daughter's curious mind?

I remembered that parents were extremely important because the relationship between them and the child was the framework for the relationship between the individual and God. And conversely, God's lordship was a model for parenting. So, if God chose to be invisible, was it a lesson for me as a parent?

For example, He was invisible, but He was not absent. People discovered God best when they were in their most desperate situations. And in normal times, He was enabling us to enjoy success and self-confidence by helping and guiding us in our actions without overriding our egos. Had this help and guidance been substituted by His infinite Will and Power always, we could not have controlled our actions, and so, we could not have developed even the notion of self.

I felt like I found a great gift for my daughter. But was this enough? Was this what she was looking for? Or part of it? Who knows? Perhaps, I should keep thinking. After all, I was her hero; I should not ruin her dreams.

I remembered how I was disappointed by some of my superheroes. In my childhood, superheroes were depicted as people who were there only in times of danger and emergencies. So, they were never put into contexts that would reveal a lack of character or a need to be cared for. But in recent times, superheroes were likely to be depicted with defects in their personalities. Even sometimes, they were shown trying to cover up those defects with their powers, making the picture even worse.

I did not want to disappoint my daughter. But as much as I was her hero, I was a human: a regular human with insufficiencies and mistakes. And, so was she. In any case, I didn't want to be remembered through my negatives. Wasn't I educated not to hit people in the face with their mistakes, but on the contrary, to cover them, if possible? Right at that moment, I saw that being invisible was the perfect way God did this for us.

If He revealed His presence every time we did something wrong, how shameful would that be?

But, whether covering a flaw or doing a favor, what crowned those good deeds was when the person who committed them didn't expect anything back. The best help was described as "done by the right hand without the left hand being aware of it." Doing favors while being invisible like angels was the ideal. So, the other person only knows that they have been covered, and that's it. They can't see anyone who is going to ask for a return by reminding them of the favor; they can't remember a face whose appearance would rekindle the regrets of the past mistakes. Their pride is not wounded, and their dignity is intact. They are left with a gratitude that can only be paid forward by doing the same for others. I thought, in this context, being invisible was another way by which God taught us benevolence and magnanimity by example.

Having gone through all these thoughts, I was guessing that I had found enough answers for my daughter. But since I had not figured out a way to deliver those answers without being visible, I was expecting her to have enough of me after a minute, and without much listening, to produce another question. I was wrong, and I was correct. She listened to me completely and attentively. Then she added:

"Today, during the exam, the teacher stood beside me for a minute. You cannot imagine what a stressful minute it was. Not that I was doing anything wrong, but seeing her made me so nervous. I remembered that you had told me that we were in an exam in this life. Then it dawned upon me that God being invisible was not only a part of the exam, but also a part of the help to success."

This time, we both smiled… until she reloaded me with:

"Then why did God give the need for self-confidence and success, if they potentially lead to arrogance?"

A STORY OF RESURRECTION

I n order to reconstruct my memory of life before the explosion, I read a lot, contemplated a lot. Finally, I was able to, at least, put the events in my past in an order. But it felt more like a history book about some person who lived centuries ago. It didn't feel like me. As I was brooding about this, I was inspired to write my story, an autobiography if you will, so that I could experience those events once more, but this time with my emotions. So here it is, the story of me:

That was our last night at the secure confines of mission control. Aside from the excitement and anxiety shaking us, there was a slight breeze of cold air keeping us on our toes. With more of us entering the launch site each second, the 20 minute countdown felt like a century.

But as people of cause, we knew to wait on our toes, even if it *was* for a century, to sacrifice our whole existence for our mission.

We were soldiers of complete commitment. We were swift and stern princes guided for dominion. Our determination to our target was far beyond any fear could reach. As long as the mission was accomplished, it didn't matter even if we all died. In the last seconds of the countdown, we were reminding each other that sooner or later, dying would be the only way to fulfill what we had promised. "All for one, one for all." Thus, we announced once more our commitment to each other and to our mission.

3, 2, 1, lift off. When I opened my eyes, I realized that we had already been rocketed away and deployed at our mission site, a.k.a. the burial site for most of us. The enemy was expecting our arrival. So, all the land was drenched with acid and other chemicals. The remainder of us quickly proceeded through the dead bodies of our fellows. We had no other choice but to survive and accomplish the mission.

Soon, we came to a strait that extended farther than we could see. Whether it had an exit farther down was unknown to us. We tried to stick together and kept going. But instead of an exit, the strait kept branching. Each time, we had to split. We just had no other way out of this situation. After many tense moments, with few other teammates, we reached the end of the branch we had taken. The bad news was that the exit was blocked. The good news was the material that blocked the exit was loose and watery. On the other side, we were stunned by the sight of a vast sea. It took our breath away. As we walked around, we saw a few other groups who had made it this far. The rest of us must have been dead by then, lost in the abyss of some dark strait.

For an instant, I was thinking that it was over and we were free to move forward. It didn't take too long before I learned how naïve I was. The enemy ambushed us right at the moment we were relaxing. That split second of rejoicing was the nourishment of our souls for the coming fight. The thunderous screams of the enemy surrounded us from all directions.

They were so much bigger than us in size that, instead of fighting, we just ran away as fast as we could. We eventually decided to gather into one group in order to protect those who were inside while the outsiders absorbed their threats and sacrificed themselves for those inside. At least, if some of us survived this calamity, it would make everyone content, even if only at the last breaths of our lives.

Right at that moment of doom, a strong wind started, and threw some of us to the entrance of a tunnel. I can tell you this because I was one of them. Others who could not catch the wind fell prey to the enemy. With each mate falling dead, the weight of our responsibility increased. It was as if we were carrying their dead bodies along with us. I didn't know whether I would die due to the unending catastrophes or whether I would be crushed under the weight of this responsibility. With the final bits of power I still had, I squeezed myself into that tunnel with the hope of reaching safe ground.

After we proceeded a little bit, I realized that there were no more enemies in the vicinity. I looked around, and realized that we were actually surrounded by food and water. Was this real or was I hallucinating? Or was I already dead and witnessing paradise? But others with me saw the same hallucination, which was impossible. It was real. I shed tears of relief and joy. Right then, as if all the beauty around us was not enough, I smelled an enthralling scent in the air. It was as if someone was trying to say welcome.

I closed my eyes and fast-forwarded from our moment of deployment to this land. We had to pass through the dark strait without knowing if and where it had an exit, and then flee a gigantic enemy with chemical weapons. Right when we were falling in their hands, we were picked up by a miraculous wind and were left at these safe grounds. Within these few hours, we had lost almost everybody. After all that, we were in this heaven. It was just incredible. But our journey was not over, and our mission was not accomplished yet.

We restarted proceeding towards the source of that scent. With the increasing intensity of the scent and the growing exhilaration it gave, some of us lost our sanity. Fortunately, not so long after, I saw some faint lights on the horizon. That was it. I was smiling like never before in my life. With a few fellows next to me, we swam wildly towards the light.

When we arrived at the final destination, I was so happy it went down to every atom of my being. I just lay on the ground, and made a prostration of gratitude. Other fellows joined me in that, but they quickly stood up and started looking for a suitable spot to penetrate inside. Me, I couldn't find any force in myself to move a single muscle, let alone get up. Perhaps this was my time. I whispered to myself: "one for all." What was going to happen after this was beyond me. In that position of prostration, I simply submitted myself to the growing explosion in my head, which buried me into my grave. And that was the end of my life.

I don't know how much time passed, but the first thing I could do afterwards was open my eyes. As a matter of fact, I did not know if I had anything else other than eyes. It must have been the explosion in my head that had erased my memory and even my awareness of myself. For a while, I lived as if I had no past. It was so adventurous; believe me.

For a long time, I wondered about those things dangling around me. Soon, I realized that I could actually control them: my arms and my legs. When I started walking, others around me burst into joy. By looking at their reactions, I could tell that I was amazing. After learning to express myself verbally, everybody chuckled whenever I said, "I am amazing, right?"

That was not the only thing that made them chuckle though. Having started doing unbelievable things and realizing how miraculous I was, I couldn't help asking, "how did I come to be?" Every time I asked that question, first I received a chuckle or a giggle, and then either a complicated answer or words of nonsense. The answer to that question was so sensitive for me, though, because something kept bothering me. Years later, I discovered biology books, and exuberantly dove into them. During one of those readings, when I read the following, a smile came to my face. I knew that I had found me and my past:

"The biological creation of a human starts with the sperms leaving the body of the male for a long and difficult journey into the female's body. The sperms first have to travel through the female's vagina and cervix, survive the acidic environment, then must flee her immune system, and finally have to search in a vast space for the entrance to the fallopian tube. Only the few who can survive all these trials have the chance to participate in the final round: breaking into the egg. The sperms who reach the egg try to find a suitable spot for penetration. Upon the contact of the membranes of the sperm and the egg and after the protein match between them, the chemicals in the sperm's head explode, following which the genetic material from the male is transferred inside the egg. Out of millions of sperm, only one of them can accomplish this mission, and this moment of success marks the end of its life."

My first reaction was "No, I am still alive!"

* * *

"Does not man see that it is We Who created him from sperm? Yet behold! He (stands forth) as an open adversary! And he makes comparisons for Us, and forgets his own creation: He says, 'Who can give life to bones and decomposed ones?' Say, 'He will give them life Who created them for the first time!' For He fully knows all!" The Holy Qur'an 36:77–79.

DESCENT FROM THE IVORY TOWER

Refugee in a tower of agony
Hungry for ceaseless beauty
In love with eternity
Refugee in a tower of agony

On an early, rainy morning
When the birds started singing
He woke to a vision crying
On an early, rainy morning

Stepping down the hill slowly
Pondering over his troubles calmly
He was seeking for a canopy
Stepping down the hill slowly

As the uncertain end nears
Rocks, trees, leaves, rivers…

None but One hears his fears
As the uncertain end nears

In need of a fundamental change
Past life and fears scream with rage
His ivory tower is no different than a cage
In need of a fundamental change

Not knowing the final destination
In the turbulent life-story ocean
Rediscovering a one-to-one relation
Descent from the ivory tower becomes Ascension

HISTORY OF RELIGION—B.C.

"In the past, people believed in God, because they could not defeat death. So, they came up with this idea of a being that is more powerful than death. But today, death is defeated. Therefore, we no longer need a being that is more powerful than death."

Despite this arrogant proclamation of the immortals, I and others like me still chose to be mortal. We continued our daily lives with our usual duties, and embraced death as the start of a larger life. From time to time, we sent messages to those infidels for them to come back to the normal order. However, they simply ignored all the warnings. Day by day, they increased in number and survived for their own sake. We died, one by one, for the sake of everyone.

Luckily, this spiral down had started at a point when we were incomparably more than them. In the beginning, they were kept in confinement so that their survival would not cause big problems for the rest of us. But, they started migrating to every corner of the universe to escape the order, and their numbers increased out of control. What is bitter is that for their migration, they used the very system that we maintained by staying where we were.

Fortunately, this outrageous state of the immortals was not ignored by the heavens. One day, an honest one among us who was respected by everyone announced that he was a Prophet. Then, he started preaching that one day this universe would come to an end. Even if you did not ever die, your life would be terminated with the devastation of the universe, he explained. So he called the immortals to abide by the order and not to create conflict and distress for the others.

The immortals' answer was simple: "we don't think that the universe will come to an end. Even if it is going to, we will find a cure for that, too." This sarcasm blended with their arrogance made their immortality ever more obnoxious.

We stayed away from them more and more. But, as we died one by one where we were, they kept increasing in number everywhere they could migrate. One day, the immortals were going to dominate this place and everywhere else.

This fact did not go unnoticed by the heavens. Soon, some miracles happened, as predicted by the Prophet. Whenever the immortals took some water to drink, it became poison. Many of them died; but not all.

After a while, the Prophet prayed for the termination of the miracle, and it was held back. Then he made a second call to the surviving immortals: "This is a sign for you. If you are mindful, take this respite as an opportunity to repent."

But instead of repentance, the arrogance of the immortals drove them even more arrogant: "We survived your miracle. It was not a miracle, after all! And we are going to outnumber you mortals again. One day, no miracle will stop us."

As the days went by, the immortals kept hiding in the distant corners of the universe, but one day, they re-emerged; this time, they were stronger than before. Their claim for immortality was undefeatable. They kept increasing in number at a faster pace, and their presence rendered our environment inhabitable. We were dying at rates never seen before. So, the survivors among us begged the Prophet to defeat the immortals once again.

This time, something totally unexpected happened. All of their colonies were devastated by a heavenly blow. Again, most of them were eliminated; but not all. The Prophet again made a call to the surviving immortals: "Don't be like your brethren. Heed what I am telling you. Come back to the order."

But the arrogance in their hearts was inexhaustible. Their answer reflected the darkness in their minds: "Those who died were simply not prepared enough. But, we again survived. We are stronger than ever before. We will outnumber you again, and one day, no event will catch us unprepared."

Although the threatening words of the immortals scared us, our hopes were fresh with the presence of the Prophet among us. But one day, something unexpected happened: as every other mortal, the Prophet died. That day, we were not only sad due to our loss but also devastated due to the mockery of the immortals: "Now who is going to save you from us?"

Day by day, we saw the immortals colonizing one more place in the universe. They kept increasing in number, and we kept dying, one by one. Life became more and more unbearable. Every one of us still alive started praying for relief. Those days, our prayers were answered by a consolation from the teachings of the Prophet: Even if you don't die ever, the universe is going to come to an end, and you are going to die with it. So we were clinging to the hope of the universe coming to an end and us being born into a fresh life.

Soon, our prayers were answered. I remember some of the things on that last day. Rivers stopped, heavens were ruptured, and everything started dying. The immortals were the strongest ones, so they survived the longest, perhaps to the last minute. But I am not sure if their survival was due to their strength or due to an extended torment for not being able to die.

....

Cancer is a disease of the cells by which they acquire the ability to reproduce uncontrollably and to avoid all signs for cell death. Their supremacy to the normal body cells is not restricted to their immortality. They also acquire an unparalleled ability to migrate to other places and to adjust to the life conditions there. The treatment of cancer today involves use of chemicals to kill the cancer cells, removal of the cancerous tissue, and inducing cell death through exposure to radiation. If untreated, the increase of these immortal cells in every corner of the body results in the disruption of the regular functioning of the systems that underlie the life of the organism. However, the malfunction of the body eventually leads to death, by which every cell is killed.

RETURN TO INNOCENCE

"**T**his is totally unacceptable! Oh my God, this is insane! Who do you think you are?" the mother shouted to her son, who was standing before her with a full bag of various items. "Get rid of 'em, quick!"

That was the mother's verdict on the issue. The poor boy did not know what to do at first. Should he give the bag back to his friend, or should he return those items to their real owners? "Either way, I am going to be doing what mom is telling me," the boy thought.

Soon, he was on his way to the local mall. Since he was not yet allowed to drive, he took the bus for this adventure. On one hand, his adolescent excitement was gushing out of him as an unstoppable smile. But then, his smile was getting smashed under the gazes of other people on the bus, whose looks seemed like arrows aimed at him.

It didn't take too long in this small town for a bus to arrive at the mall. His heart was beating so wildly that he feared it would break through his chest. He could barely utter a word; how could he explain the situation to the owners and apologize? Meanwhile, he found himself going to the shop to which the cheapest item in the bag belonged.

This shop was towards the center of the mall and was packed with lots of small items. You could play hide-and-seek here without even once being found. But all those crevices in the store were not enough to veil the boy's red face among other people. He approached one of the clerks, pulled the item out of the bag, and opened his mouth to say … no, nothing could come out through his lips; it was as if his words were blocked by that ball in his throat! He had to force that ball down into his stomach, but it made him sick in the stomach. Then he heard a kind sentence:

"Are you returning this, honey?"

He simply nodded.

"Do you have your receipt?"

"No, but I don't want money back. It belongs here!"

"Let me see it. Hmmm, this indeed belongs to this store. I will place it in the shelf, and I appreciate your honesty." Then she stretched her hand to the boy. They shook hands, and the boy left the store with relief on his face.

Then he took a few seconds to quell his heart beats. Now, he was standing on firmer ground to proceed with the other items in the bag. He looked back to the store he just left. That lady was explaining something to another clerk while pointing at him. He wanted to get away before things changed for the worse.

He took another deep breath, and started pacing towards the second target on his list of deliveries. He suddenly thought about Santa Clause. "But he doesn't return stolen items ..." he thought.

The second store sold somewhat more expensive home utility tools. It was certainly bigger than the previous one, with fewer crevices in which to hide. It took a while for the boy to find a clerk with the least scary face: another lady. She was probably in her late thirties. Her face was not scary, but her look was very serious. "I hope she didn't fight with her husband last night," the boy thought.

He pulled out the items that belonged to this store, and the same conversation started:

"I am returning these items!"

"Do you have your receipt?"

"No, but I don't need the money back! These belong here!"

The clerk looked puzzled: "What do you mean these belong to here?"

"They were taken from here, and I am returning them!"

The lady asked the boy to wait at the register for a second, and turned her back to go inside the store. Her walk was actually more like a triumphant commander entering the city that she kept under siege for a long time.

"You, little serpent! You are going to pay for what you made me go through."

She had been penalized for not being able to stop the shoplifting that was going on for the past month. Soon, the lady came back with the manager. And just after them, came the security officers of the mall through the entrance.

The boy burst into an out loud cry and kept repeating the same sentence whenever he was able to control his hick-ups: "I didn't do it, I didn't do it." He soon was in the grip of the security officers, which felt like concrete cuffs. The entire mall was echoing with his cry: "I didn't do it."

In the main security office, the chief opened the bag, and asked the other officers:

"Are these also on the stolen items list?"

"Yes, sir."

The boy repeated again: "I didn't do anything wrong," only to hear: "We know, we know!" That felt like a fist that entered the boy's throat down to his stomach. The chief officer asked about the contact information of his parents, but he refused to answer. It was his mother, in the first place, who was the cause of his being in this situation. Instead, he tried his best to take another breath, and asked the chief officer to listen to him. Upon approval, he explained:

"A friend of mine took these items with the intention of returning them later, but he couldn't. So, I decided to do this on his behalf."

"Is there evidence that what you are telling me is true?" asked the chief officer. Just then, another officer came in, and reported that the kid was also recognized in the security camera records. "But, we saw a second boy with this one, who was carrying the bag" added the same officer.

The chief officer couldn't make up his mind about the situation. Other than suspicion, there was no solid evidence to prove this kid guilty. As a matter of fact, they could be ruining the angel-like heart of this boy by judging according to their suspicion.

But, still there was a chance that the two boys were collaborators. If that was the case, then it would be most appropriate to find the parents and send the boy to a "safe place." The chief asked the boy to tell the story again. Maybe he could find some discrepancies among the versions, and could substantiate his suspicions. The boy repeated the same story; but this time in an unexpected version:

"My friend always wanted to earn a lot of money. If he did so, he could go away with his mom and his siblings to some place, where they would not be disturbed by cops that are trying to catch his oldest brother. That's how he got into the rental business. I tried to explain to him that it was wrong to take things that belonged to someone else. But he always said that those items stayed on the shelf for so long that even their owners must have forgotten about them. After all, he was only renting them to other people for a little time, but not owning them. Yesterday, the cops captured his brother finally, and I was afraid that the same would happen to my friend, too. Seeing his brother being taken by the cops scared him so much that he couldn't come back to return the rental items. So, I decided to do it for him."

The chief officer concluded that he was barking up the wrong tree. He sent another officer to accompany the boy while he returned the rest of the rental items to be placed in their spots in the shelves to rest in peace.

SEPARATION

H ave you ever thought of the mechanics of a murder? Yes, the mechanics of a murder! Given a 50 gram-mass at point A with a velocity of 400 m/s, the time it takes to reach point B that is 4 meters away is approximately 10 milliseconds. When this mass reaches point B, it contacts a surface that can sustain a maximum of 90 m/s² acceleration. Because the momentum of the 50 gram-mass is high enough to overcome this limit, it penetrates this surface. As it cuts through the target object, its kinetic energy is converted to heat. Eventually, the moving object comes to a stop, but the path it has opened, now becomes filled with a red-colored fluid whose density is 1060 kg/m³ and whose viscosity is 3.5 x 10—3 Pa·s. When this fluid flow stops due to a process called agglutination, or commonly known as clotting, the whole system achieves the steady-state behavior, i.e. all motions come to a halt.

"All motions come to a halt"; that is death. This explanation could be the murder of your parent who was assassinated while working for the good of your country; or your family members who were martyred during a war. And this scientific picture made of dead words cannot portray the love and sorrow gushing out of your eyes. But I can tell you where your love and sorrow can be found.

Loving means being vulnerable, and you know why? Because when you love someone, their presence stimulates the release of dopamine in your brain. Dopamine is the hormone that lowers the threshold for feeling pleasure and pain, thus you feel pleased and hurt more easily. Your emotional devastation is nothing but an accumulation of dopamine in your brain. Just wait until it diffuses completely. As the common wisdom says: Time heals everything.

Loving also means bonding, and you know why? Because when you love someone, their presence stimulates the release of oxytocin in your body. Oxytocin is the hormone that accompanies the feeling of serenity while with your loved one. It also functions in pair bonding and fidelity. Your terror in mind and brokenness in soul in the aftermath of your loss is only a hunger for oxytocin.

What did you say? My explanations would not console you? See a psychiatrist, and take some pills to balance your hormone levels. Don't worry. Everything is going to be all right.

...

THAT'S ENOUGH!

...

I cannot take it anymore. I can't go on with my life when one side of my being is tortured by the other. Did you, too, feel tormented by the explanations I just told you? These words are coming from the cold chamber of science where all emotions are to be kept dead-frozen. Isn't it a murder in itself?

I am an aerodynamicist. Calling myself an aerodynamicist recalls an ideology that hasn't been named, that doesn't exist in encyclopedias: aerodynamicism. Aerodynamicism has its own dogmas, rules, methods. It tells you that air is just another fluid whose behavior can be studied through mathematics and experiments. So, I ask myself, by subscribing to aerodynamicism and providing mechanical explanations devoid of conscience, am I committing a murder against air? What if the air's motion is the embodiment of conscious acts with feelings?

Perhaps I should listen to air itself, instead of what others say about it. Maybe I should at least give air a chance to show me that it is actually alive, that it has emotions. So I stand atop a hill overlooking a bay. I keep silent, and try to remove the scientific knowledge that is clogging my ears. And I start hearing something:

It is the wind. As the air approaches my body, it slows down, forms a stationary layer right around my torso. Around this layer, it paces gradually towards my back. Behind my arms, it forms small vortices that are shed along with the wind. What I am hearing is actually the sound from the friction between my ear and the air. And the whistling sound is the vortex-shedding triggered by the separation of the air flow from the body surface.

Hey, hey, hey … I thought I was listening to the air. This is not air! This is my self, forging mechanical shapes and passing them off as if they belong to air. If air has feelings, it must be very disappointed by my hypocritical pose of listening. I just invited it into my lungs for an intimate conversation, but I aborted it with my scientific thoughts.

I should apologize. My eyes closed, arms wide-open, I allow my whole being to be embraced by air. "I am sorry. I hope I did not hurt your feelings. Are you crying?"

"Crying only ends with the act of shedding tears; but it starts long before when someone hurts the love inherent in the creation. I am crying. I want to shed my tears, each like a galaxy, to the expanse of the universe till the end of time. Isn't there someone to hear me out there?"

"Why do you feel so alone?"

"I feel alone because I am different. Although I visit many people, many places every day, it is a very routine interaction going on between me and everything else: mundane tasks to be performed without intimacy. Like the two parties in a business. Once the mutual interests are delivered, the relationship is over. No loyalty, no love. I imagine myself like a chunk of meat going through a meat grinder. This is a meaningless, merciless flow where your identity or existence means nothing special. So, why would I talk to those people about my private world anyway? Instead, just a few words about the weather…"

"I wish I could do something for you!"

"The Creator didn't give me eyes so that I would embrace everyone, good or bad; so that every individual in this world is cared for. So, I would like to become friends and feel the warmth of their presence. Often I ask myself when they are going to realize that I am offering my love by hugging them. At least, I wish they saw my tears upon separation from them …"

I didn't consider air a living being to start with! But now, I was learning that air was hugging me! And was it crying, too? Could the mechanical explanations be blinding me to the reality behind the observations? In this case, the no-slip condition was nothing but air hugging a loved one. And flow separation and vortex shedding were actually manifestations of a sorrow of separation. How is it possible that I am so distant to someone that is so close to me?

My turbulence inside exhibited itself as a silence outside. At least, so I thought. But I couldn't be farther from reality.

"I am used to this kind of silence. Despite their nonchalance towards me, I still care a lot about people. And using the subtle clues in their words and voices, I can penetrate into their psyche."

Someone who knows me better than I? And I can't even see that someone! When and how have I become its focus of attention?

"With their first breaths and cries, I start observing them from within."

From within?

"With every breath, I become part of their souls, and with every utterance, I am part of their connections. Through the subtle clues in their voices and words, I learn about their emotions. Thus I feel even the pains they are ardently hiding from their selves. As I leave them in that state, I break into a thousand pieces. But, the Creator made me invisible. So, none of what I learn about them is revealed to the eyes of strangers. Thus, I make a reticent friend."

I was totally conquered by these words. I found myself whispering "Not just reticent! You are a reticent and affectionate companion that anyone would like to have."

"People live by breathing, and I breathe by loving; loving even if there is no reciprocity. As life goes on, I think about new people to be relieved of their pain ... Even if they won't take me as one among them ..."

"I love you air, I love you ..."

FREEDOM—MADE ON EARTH

Working in a hospital is as thought provoking as it is overwhelming. Actually, the thoughts that flock into your mind are no less overwhelming than the work, either. Seeing a man with a complete leg replacement, or a lady surviving on an artificial heart, forces me to think of the end of the road. What is going to happen if we continue replacing all parts of the body in order to live longer?

There was this old man today. The doctor recommended he exercise regularly, in order to conserve his bone strength. Alas for him, the good old days are gone. He is not the young, energetic man he used to be; once, he could squeeze the water out of stone! But now? He needs to exercise and use several pills to escape the numerous ailments trying to invade his body. The good old days … Really, what would it be like if you were an old man in the old days?

I remember my grandfather. He was a tough man; you had to extract the joy out of him. But still, he meant something special. He used to hold us in his arms, make tricks to entertain us, and we would laugh and flock around him to figure out how he did them. We used to work in the garden together, and then swim away in the sea together, reaching the deep places; and that would be our secret, not to be told to mom. We used to do the weekly shopping together, and carry heavy bags of good stuff from the bazaar. I used to fear that I was going to be reprimanded for the eggs I broke on the way. But regardless, I was special to him, and he was special to me.

Coming back to today, an old man runs in a park or walks on a treadmill all by himself. He swings dead masses of iron up and down. He watches the comic movies to laugh. He goes to the psychologist to talk to someone, and if that is not enough, he takes antidepressants to keep his sanity. If he direly needs the youngsters around him, he falls sick, since people only gather anymore if there is an emergency. At times, his different body parts are operated on or replaced. The old man is not special to his caregivers, nor are his caregivers special to him. When his family one day consults the doctors about him, they say, "it is the old age."

As for the grandchildren, their grandfather is replaced by the never-ending storyteller—TV. But the children are not special to this storyteller, nor is this story-teller special to the children. Their emotions are not stimulated by a grandfather, but dictated through incessant songs. They don't ever fear being reprimanded by the TV, but their addiction to it keeps them from embracing life with its ups and downs. When you try to circumvent this unhealthy fixation, they consider you to be interfering with their freedom. If not being special is freedom, I think we should rename it free-doom.

TELESCOPES AND MICROSCOPES

For among rocks there are some from which rivers gush forth; others there are which when split asunder send forth water; and others which sink for fear of Allah.

The Holy Qur'an (2:74)

And neither heaven nor earth shed a tear over them;

The Holy Qur'an (44:29)

The seven heavens and the earth, and all beings therein, declare His glory: There is not a thing but celebrates His praise; And yet you understand not how they declare His glory!

The Holy Qur'an (17:44)

[All] praise is [due] to Allah. He will show you His signs, and you will recognize them.

The Holy Qur'an (27:93)

And how many Signs in the heavens and the earth do they pass by? Yet they turn (their faces) away from them!

The Holy Qur'an (12:105)

Translations from Abdullah Yusuf Ali and Sahih International